"With some practice, kissing can look enough like love to convince anyone."

Laura shook her head and withdrew as much as the seats would allow. "I don't need practice."

He leaned toward her until their faces were mere inches apart, his voice turning to liquid silver as he murmured, "What are you afraid of?"

"Afraid?" She forced the words out on a trilling laugh while she pressed back into her seat, trying to create space between them while her hands gripped the armrests. "I'm not afraid."

Kyros reacted to her claim with a knowing smile, the unnerving calm of his voice a marked contrast to the simmering tension in his big body. "Maybe you should be."

"I'm not," she scoffed while her pulse clamored wildly within her ears. "Kissing is kissing." She tried to dismiss him with a haughty arch of her brow. "I'm sorry if that bruises your fragile ego, but one man is the same as another. I don't have to *practice* to prove that to you."

"You obviously haven't kissed enough men," he purred while his fingers rose to stroke the ridge of her jaw.

NATASHA TATE's romantic side has its roots in childhood. Ask anyone and you'll hear she spent too many of her formative years believing she was Cinderella. This despite the fact that she had two loving parents and no evil stepmother in sight. Her earliest drawings were of princess attire, replete with bows, ribbons and multiple flounces. She warbled about her future prince during chores and began each night by assuming the most earnest Sleeping Beauty pose.

Alas, school did not tolerate such fanciful notions, and she quickly learned to rely on romance novels to satisfy her cravings for happy endings. As an army brat and perennial new kid she consumed a book a day, hiding them within her textbooks while training half an ear on her teachers' lectures. This habit persisted into college, despite her more traditional academic pursuits, equipping her with the skills needed to tame her own alpha male hero.

Now that she's married and the mother of three strapping sons, Natasha's experiencing her own happily ever after. As an author for Harlequin Books, she lives her dream of crafting fairy-tale romances set in modern-day, larger-than-life settings. Visit her at www.NatashaTate.com, or email her at Natasha@NatashaTate.com.

Other titles by Natasha Tate available in eBook

Harlequin Presents®

A WORLD SHE DOESN'T BELONG TO

NATASHA TATE

~ **A Deal with the Devil** ~

TORONTO NEW YORK LONDON
AMSTERDAM PARIS SYDNEY HAMBURG
STOCKHOLM ATHENS TOKYO MILAN MADRID
PRAGUE WARSAW BUDAPEST AUCKLAND

Recycling programs
for this product may
not exist in your area.

ISBN-13: 978-0-373-52874-5

A WORLD SHE DOESN'T BELONG TO

This edition published by arrangement with Harlequin Books S.A.

For questions and comments about the quality of this book
please contact us at Customer_eCare@Harlequin.ca.

® and TM are trademarks of the publisher. Trademarks indicated with
® are registered in the United States Patent and Trademark Office, the
Canadian Trade Marks Office and in other countries.

www.Harlequin.com

Printed in U.S.A.

A WORLD SHE
DOESN'T BELONG TO

To my dearest CP and longtime friend,
Jennie Lucas. Thank you for convincing me
that families can survive when mothers pursue
their dreams!

CHAPTER ONE

TEN MONTHS was too damned long to go without a woman.

That was the only explanation Kyros Spyridis could think of to rationalize his reaction to his wife's presence in the New York Medical Examiner's office. It certainly wasn't the setting. Sterile white and beige, underscored with medicine, astringent and the scent of dirty snow, was no aphrodisiac. And it couldn't have been the discovery that Lana was still miraculously alive after her accident.

No.

He wouldn't lie to himself about that. Not when the news of her death had triggered an undeniable flash of relief.

His bride hadn't even waited six weeks after their son's birth before she was trolling for a new party, a new lover, and a new way to spend the money marriage to him provided. Given her self-absorbed commitment to *fun,* it had been hard to muster any degree of grief at all.

Perhaps it was because he'd already suspected the truth. Lana was like a cat. She always landed on her feet: sleek, unruffled and unrepentant, no matter the circumstances.

The fact that she'd survived the explosion without a scratch didn't surprise him.

What did surprise him, though, was his body's leaping response to her obvious health.

He did *not* want to be attracted to the woman he'd mar-

ried. Anger rose to augment the heat of his arousal, fueled
by the thought of her most recent infidelity. His jaw flexed
as he stared at Lana's profile. If she and her lover had suffered such a *fatal* accident, then why was she here, looking
so glaringly intact? And why the hell was *he* here, dragged
halfway around the world when she wasn't even hurt?

Irritated by his response to her, by the coil of warmth
gathering in his groin, he studied her as she stood beneath
the harsh white lights, trying to divine what, exactly, had set
off the surge of attraction he hadn't felt since the first time
he'd seen her.

He'd been drunk that fateful night nearly a year ago, in
the mood to celebrate his latest merger and too inebriated to
see beyond the gorgeous package to the conniving little gold
digger lurking beneath the surface.

Unfortunately, by the time he'd figured out his error of
judgment, it had been too late. The damage had already been
done.

He still couldn't figure out how it had happened. Even
when he was drunk, he *never* forgot protection. But the DNA
test Kyros had demanded proved Lana right: she was pregnant with his son, leaving him with only one choice to differentiate himself from the man who'd fathered him.

One choice to keep his grandmother's faith in him intact.

Giagiá had never blamed him for the death of his mother
or the sins of his amoral father; she'd loved him, supported
him and raised him to be a man of honor despite his flawed
genetics.

He'd die before he proved her wrong.

So he'd married the spoiled, manipulative American.
Without a word of complaint, he'd endured nine months of
marital misery with a woman he couldn't abide.

Granted, Lana was as beautiful as she'd always been, an
enchanting blend of blue-eyed minx and ballerina, with up-
swept sable hair and a pale blush of pink lending color to her

cheeks. But he was no longer fooled by the exterior trappings of the woman he'd married. The subtle underpinnings of passion that simmered beneath her innocent smiles, beckoning men like a siren's song, didn't work on him, either. He was immune to her charms.

He *was,* damn it all.

He watched her in silence as he drew near, suppressing his sexual awareness with a brutal force of will. *Think of Titus,* he ordered himself. *Think of what a wretched mother she is to your son.*

For some reason, the admonitions didn't work.

Narrowing his eyes, he catalogued her fragile, bowed posture with a grim frown. With her delicate body wrapped in a wool coat the color of weak tea, he was surprised to discover she'd traded out her usual flashy style for a conservative skirt and heels. Something was different, he realized, as he drew to a stop a few meters away. He'd never seen his wife look so…small.

Perhaps it was the brush with death that had changed her.

No. He dismissed the thought without further internal debate. Lana would never be introspective enough to learn or grow from the experience of an accident that had left her unscathed. If anything, she'd have been annoyed that the party aboard her lover's yacht had been interrupted by an inconvenient engine explosion.

Lana must have sensed his presence because she turned to face him, inhaling sharply while her slender hand flew up to press against her throat.

Kyros froze, the startling juxtaposition of what he read in Lana's face and what he'd expected to find making his gut twist. What game was she playing now? And why did her expression look so stricken and raw?

If he didn't know better, he'd think Lana was consumed by a debilitating grief, her composure hanging on by a mere thread.

He gave himself a mental shake. Lana? Grieving? Impossible.

Lana didn't care about anything or anyone enough to grieve.

But then why…?

Fingers of unease gripped the base of his spine as Kyros fought the irrational urge to gather his wife close, to kiss the sorrow from her quivering mouth and murmur reassurances into the delicate shell of her ear.

He cleared his throat and remained where he stood, suddenly aware of how constricting his suit and tie felt. "What's going on here?" he asked with a scowl.

Her clear eyes, glimmering with a disconcerting blend of innocence and tears, widened. "You don't know?" she asked in a thin, tremulous voice.

Kyros had thought himself incapable of being surprised, least of all by Lana. But the fact that her statement communicated confusion instead of its typical haughty dismissal astonished him.

Irritated, he growled, "I don't have time to travel halfway around the world to clean up yet another of your *accidents*."

"Another of *my*…?" she stammered, looking nothing like the entitled socialite who spent more on spa treatments than most companies made in a year. Her brow furrowed before she gasped softly and then raised her palm to her chest. "Oh, no. You don't understand. I'm not—"

"I'm not interested," he interrupted as he stepped toward her and reached for her elbow. Spinning her toward the exit, he marched her forward. "I have a business to run and employees to oversee. You're alive and I'm taking you home. Now."

"No!" Lana blurted, yanking her arm free before they'd made it ten steps. She cupped a hand around her elbow and looked up at him with the wide eyes of a troubled ingénue. "You don't understand! I'm not who you think I am."

He flicked an irritated glance at her face. "Don't be ridiculous," he said, even as her scent, an unfamiliar blend of innocence and allure she'd surely paid a fortune of his money to have blended, threatened to turn the blood in his veins to steam.

"I'm not," she insisted, her eyes suddenly awash with nervousness and something dangerously close to sympathy. Her tongue stole out to dampen the delectable seam of her mouth. "I'm Laura. Lana's twin."

"Right," he said in a clipped tone as he glared down at his wife, "the orphan I married, the woman who swore she was all alone in the world, suddenly has an identical twin. Convenient, don't you think?"

A flicker of hurt clouded her features, but she quickly hid it with a swift blink of her blue eyes. "Lana said that?"

"No. *You* said that."

"I didn't," she said, while the beat of her pulse fluttered visibly at the base of her throat. "I'm not Lana."

Against his volition, his attention shifted to trace the gentle curve of her cheek and the scattering of freckles atop the bridge of her nose. Her pink mouth trembled beneath his gaze, sending a torrent of unwanted desire coursing through him. Unnerved and feeling horrifically off-kilter, he watched as a delicate blush rose to stain Lana's skin. "You're lying," he ground out.

"I don't lie." A frown gathered between her dark brows. "Ever."

The claim was so outrageous that he laughed. It was a low and scratchy sound, one he made far too infrequently. "All you *ever* do is lie," he accused as he stepped closer. Towering over her, trying to intimidate her into telling the truth for once in her wretched, selfish, little life, he waited until her indignant frown wavered into a trembling line of nervousness.

"I'm…I'm not lying." Emotion flashed behind her clear

gaze of sea blue, but it vanished before he could catalogue it properly. "Lana might have, but I wouldn't. I swear."

He narrowed his eyes. Was that a hint of confused vulnerability he'd read in her expression? His fists clenched as he brushed the irrational thought aside. Lana was about as vulnerable as a viper, and he'd be smart to remember it. He'd be even smarter if he could make his *body* remember it. "Don't think I'll believe you just because you've decided to reinvent yourself. Again."

Lana swallowed, drawing his gaze to the delicate column of her white throat. "I don't blame you for doubting me. Lana did have a tendency to…get creative at times." The slight breathlessness in her delivery made it sound as if she were as disturbed by their proximity as he. "But this is not one of those times. I promise."

Determined to regain control of his unwieldy libido, he stood his ground and waited for her to back down, hoping she'd react to his nearness the way she always did. He needed her to be impatient with his interference, to remind him that this unwelcome fascination was an aberration unworthy of his attention.

Instead, she merely waited, her breath shallow and her blue eyes carefully searching his. The overhead lights glinted on the tips of her eyelashes and fired her sleek brunette hair with glimmers of mahogany and wine. His fingers itched to reach for her, to drag her up and kiss her lush mouth back into its perpetual pout.

No.

Lana was a spoiled, manipulative harpy who deserved nothing beyond his cold disdain.

He lifted his wrist to check his watch. "I don't have time for this. We're leaving. And you're coming with me."

"No."

"Yes. We have Christmas on the island in three days," he

reminded her, "and it appears you need a refresher course on how to play the role of my obedient, besotted wife."

"I told you. I'm not your wife. Lana is. *Was,*" she corrected.

Anger coiled deep in his gut. "Don't think this little game of yours will excuse you from the holidays with *Giagiá,*" he said on a flare of nostril. "We made a deal, remember?"

"I never made any deal with you," she insisted, stumbling backward to create more space between them while nervousness pulled at her mouth.

Too irritated to tolerate her stalling tactics, he reached for her while she shrank back in obvious fear.

Fear? What the hell did she have to be afraid of? "Knock it off," he told her as he gripped her upper arms. "I don't believe you, so you may as well stop the act," he said as he fought the urge to shake the truth from her.

Her hands flew up between them, and the press of her small fingers against his chest sent sharp spikes of awareness along his nerve endings. "It's not an act!" she protested.

Dumbfounded at his reaction to her small body twisting against his hands, he tried to stem the tide of explicit images crowding his brain while his groin tightened in eager readiness. He imagined her pressed flush against the sterile white wall, her skirt rucked up and her panties ripped aside. He saw her blushing torso bared to his hungry gaze, the tidy line of buttons on her uncharacteristically prim brown suit torn asunder. He wanted to bite the tips of her pink-and-ivory breasts, to trace her fragile lattice of rib with his fingers and tongue. He ached to spread her slim thighs and plunder her slick folds with his mouth until she panted and screamed and clutched at his hair with both hands.

"Go look at her," she begged while an edge of panic colored her voice. "Please. See for yourself."

He yanked his hands free and shoved aside his arousal with a surge of self-disgust. He would *not* allow her to ma-

nipulate him again. "What'd you do, seduce some sap into creating a convincing scene for you?"

"What?" she gasped.

Studying her impassioned features, he battled the thread of doubt that threatened his conviction. It wasn't like Lana to allow her emotions to get the best of her. But it wasn't like her to ignore the details, either. Lana could exploit any situation to her advantage, and he'd be a fool to forget it. "I wouldn't put anything past you, Lana."

"I told you!" she said while her blue eyes glittered with distress. "I am *not* Lana!"

"So you keep saying," he said in condemnation, taking note of the way emotion had painted the crests of her cheek a heated pink. "And I must admit, the blush is especially convincing."

The pink deepened to red while she opened her brown handbag and started rummaging. "I can prove it to you."

"Anything you pull out of that bag could have been bought," he informed her. "With *my* money."

She stopped her rummaging and gaped up at him. "Are you always this callous?"

Kyros cocked a sardonic brow. "Considering the hell you've put me through this year, I'd say I'm being remarkably pleasant about the fact that you're still alive."

Her sharp inhale rent the air. "How can you say such a horrible thing about your wife, the woman you *loved*?"

"I never loved you, and you damn well know it."

"You never…?" she repeated, managing to look both shocked and horrified. "Why on earth would you marry Lana if you didn't love her?"

Enraged by the time he was wasting here, arguing with a woman who'd woven an entire life out of deception, he reached for her arm and wrenched her toward the hospital room she'd vacated. "Enough!" he barked as he marched her back down the hall. "If I have to look at the so-called re-

mains of my wife to get you to abandon this ridiculous story of yours, I'll look. But once I have, we're leaving without another word of protest from you. Understood?"

Yanking the green curtain aside, he strode toward the metal table and jerked the white sheet back from the body laid out upon its dull aluminum surface.

A dizzying sense of vertigo threatened his balance and weakened his legs as he stared down at the battered face and limbs he'd have recognized anywhere.

Theos.

Lana *did* have a twin.

CHAPTER TWO

LAURA STRUGGLED to catch her breath, her heart thundering within her chest as Kyros Spyridis slowly turned back to her. "See?" she told the imposing man who'd married her sister. "I told you I'm not your wife. I'm Laura. Laura Talbot."

His mouth pressed into a grim white line as he turned back to glare down at Lana's still body.

"I'm sorry," she told his tight profile.

He didn't answer, his jaw flexing as he gripped the edge of the table.

"They assured me she felt no pain," Laura offered. "That when the explosion—"

"Don't—" He cut himself off, inhaled and then shifted to drag the white sheet back up over Lana's head. "I need a minute."

"Of course," she murmured as she dipped her head and wrapped her arms around her ribs. She didn't know the first thing about consoling the brother-in-law she'd only read about in gossip magazines. She didn't know how she was supposed to feel or act, and she felt guilty that her thoughts kept straying to him instead of toward the sister she hadn't heard from in nearly a decade.

Laura still didn't understand why Lana had always been so unhappy, why nothing had ever been enough. Her twin had always wanted more than she, their mother, and their small

Oregon town could provide. She'd wanted more excitement, more adventure, more money, more…more.

Laura thought Lana had finally found the *more* she'd wanted when she'd met Kyros Spyridis. Photos and speculation about Lana and the Greek banking billionaire's whirlwind courtship had graced the covers of every tabloid for over a month, and Lana had appeared deliriously happy in every picture. When the newlyweds had disappeared from the social scene and retreated to Kyros's secluded estate in Athens, Laura had hoped that marital bliss had finally brought Lana a measure of peace and contentment.

But now? Now, she realized she'd been overly optimistic. Given Kyros's reaction to *her,* when he'd thought she was Lana, it was obvious that theirs had not been a happy union.

But why would Kyros have married her when he didn't love her? When it felt as if he'd *hated* her? The lean, harsh man who'd accused her of lying had oozed contempt, and the sting of accusation in his words had lashed at her sensitive flesh with no hint of mercy.

Laura stole another glance at Kyros's averted profile, his body so tense and still he seemed to be a sculpture cleaved from granite.

He must have married Lana because he'd been blinded by attraction. Because when he'd looked at *her* with banked hunger in his pale green eyes, Laura had felt as if he was a ravenous predator and she was his next meal. He'd glowered at her as if he couldn't decide whether to wring her neck or ravish her into insensate, breathless submission.

Though Laura had seen countless men stare at her sister that way, it was also the first time such scalding desire had been directed at her. It was the first time her own awareness of a handsome, virile man in his prime had completely eroded her common sense.

And yet it had. Undeniably so. She'd seen his tall frame, and her body had reacted without regard to the propriety of

the situation. Against her better judgment, she'd felt herself heat with awareness. With a wholly inappropriate and *wrong* longing for what could never be hers.

One simmering glance from him, and she'd forgotten entirely that she was in New York to identify her sister's body. She'd forgotten her reason for coming, forgotten about her grief, forgotten how to breathe.

The fact that she was *still* struggling to remember why he was here, why they were *both* here, filled her with self-reproach and a flood of guilt. She had to be the worst person to ever walk the earth. It didn't matter that she hadn't talked to Lana in almost ten years. She was her *sister*! The only family she'd had left.

The reminder brought a lump of self-recrimination to her throat.

"Who else knows this is Lana?" Kyros asked, angling a glance toward Laura and interrupting her thoughts. "Who else have you told?"

"No one," she admitted while she grappled with her guilt. "I only spoke with the medical examiner. He needed me to identify her."

"How did he know to contact you when I didn't even know you existed?"

She flinched at his sharp tone, at the unspoken judgment underlying his words. "I don't know. I imagine Lana kept my number somewhere in her cell phone."

"Where is the medical examiner now?" he asked, his voice sounding clipped and angry.

"Gathering the paperwork."

Harsh and austere, his hard jade eyes trapped hers. "What paperwork?"

"Paperwork to release Lana to the…" She swallowed and looked back at her hands, wondering if her sister's husband felt *anything* for his departed wife. "To the funeral home we select."

"We'll wait for him in the hall," he said as he directed her back into the hallway. "You're looking a little pale."

Beneath the glaring fluorescent lights, Laura hauled in a deep breath and tried to quell the trembling of her mouth. Her sister's husband continued to steady her with his large, square hand, his stalwart presence an unexpected support.

"Do you know Lana's wishes regarding burial?" he eventually asked once she'd marshaled her control.

Laura bit her lip and shook her head.

"Will we need to transport her to a cemetery near your home?"

"No." Thinking of how eager Lana had been to escape the small Oregon town of her birth, Laura said, "She hated it there."

"Then we'll bury her here."

Startled, Laura lifted her gaze to his. "Here? Why not Greece?"

A small muscle ticked in his jaw. "Because she hated it there, too."

"Oh."

"It appears she wanted more than either of us could provide," he continued with a flat, emotionless voice. "So unless you have some objection, we'll allow New York to be her final resting place."

The next forty-eight hours passed in a dizzying whirlwind of preparations and stinging snow, with Laura feeling as if she were being carried along by the winter storm that was Kyros. She'd watched dumbfounded as he arranged Lana's funeral with the same degree of efficiency that he obviously brought to everything in his life.

Now, standing alone with Kyros and a shivering priest while ominous gray clouds crouched overhead and bitter winds whipped their coats about their legs, Laura found it hard to concentrate on the minister as he ushered Lana into

her eternal rest. Laura's thoughts kept straying to Kyros and all the things she'd discovered about him during the two days they'd spent together. It was no wonder he was so successful. He donned command the way other people donned shoes, and there wasn't a single person who dared to defy him, no matter how outrageous his demands.

The funeral he'd arranged, on Christmas Eve of all days, was everything Laura imagined her sister would have wanted, complete with a casket of exotic wood, the most expensive plot available and enough poinsettias to empty every florist shop within a fifty-mile radius. The only thing Kyros had failed to do was invite a posh, vibrant crowd of suitably attired mourners and friends. Not daring to ask why he'd opted for such a small, private affair when Lana had always preferred to make her exits in the most dramatic way possible, Laura stood at his side in silence as her twin was slowly lowered into the frozen ground.

When the short service ended, Laura didn't move. For several long minutes, she stared down at her sister's casket through blurred eyes while regrets and what-ifs clamored within her chest. She was all alone in the world. Momma was gone. Lana was gone. And knowing she had no family—none at all—made her throat choke with tears.

"Laura," Kyros eventually said. "You need to get out of the cold."

Laura shook her head and remained where she stood despite her numb feet. "You go. I'm fine."

Kyros moved closer, his gloved hand cupping her elbow as he stared down at her face. "She's gone. Standing out here until you freeze won't bring her back."

Knowing he was right but unwilling to abandon her final link to family, Laura bit her lip and blinked until her tears spilled over onto her chilled cheeks.

"Come," he said gently as he slowly ushered her toward the cemetery's tall iron gate.

She sniffed and watched her feet as they exited to the narrow road where his driver had parked. "Thank you for arranging such a lovely funeral," she finally said.

His curt acknowledgment was anything but warm.

"I know you didn't love her. You could have spent far less, but you gave Lana the funeral she would have wanted."

His mouth tightened. "She was my wife."

"Yes." Laura's footsteps stalled as she turned back to stare at the plot of ground now housing her sister. "She was."

"Come," he repeated as he guided her toward his waiting limousine. "We have a flight to catch."

Distracted from her thoughts of Lana, she looked up at her twin's widower in confusion. "We?"

"Yes," he said as his hand rose to press against her upper back. "Our flight leaves in an hour."

She resisted his attempt to usher her forward, her brow furrowing. "But my flight doesn't leave until tomorrow."

"Your plans have changed," said Kyros.

"My plans have...what?" she protested, pushing away his hand as he unceremoniously deposited her in his waiting limousine. "You can't just—"

"Take us to the airport," Kyros told his driver without even acknowledging Laura's words. He slid in next to her, his big body pushing hers farther into the car until he could close the door on her attempts to escape.

"No!" Laura gasped as she lunged for the door handle while the limousine rolled into motion. "I haven't—"

"Laura," Kyros said quietly, again in that tone of command she'd come to expect from him. "Relax. I had your things collected and I'll return you home after the holidays, no worse for the wear. Until then, though, I need you to pretend you're Lana."

"Pretend I'm..." She shifted back into her seat and gaped at Kyros as if he'd just told her he planned to amputate her arm. "What?"

His pale green eyes met hers with a level stare. "I'd like to hire you to pretend to be Lana for the holidays."

Stunned, Laura could do nothing but stare at his implacable face for a good minute while his limousine driver wove through traffic on its way to the airport. "You can't be serious," she said when she managed to gain her voice. "We've barely laid my sister—your *wife*—to rest, and yet you want me to pretend to be…"

"Yes."

"Are you mad?"

"I'll make it worth your while," he said as he removed the black leather gloves from his large, square hands and then tucked them inside the briefcase he'd left on the opposite seat.

"I don't want you to—"

"How much?"

"How much?" she repeated, gaping at him. There was no possible way she would accept. Not now. Not ever. "You can't pay me to pretend to be Lana! What kind of person do you think I am?"

He settled back and turned to face her, his calm eyes betraying none of his thoughts. "Would five hundred thousand dollars be enough?" he asked, as if brokering deals for half a million dollars were an everyday occurrence.

"Five hundred thousand…?" The amount was staggering, enough to pay off all Momma's hospital and funeral bills. It was enough to start again, to build a life out of the pitiful scraps that remained.

"Is that not enough?" Kyros asked, as if the amount were so paltry a sum he expected her to bargain for more.

"No," she said, shaking off the temptation to embrace the lie he wished to purchase from her.

"Seven hundred fifty," he countered, as coolly as if he were bartering for a cast-off couch at the thrift store.

She sucked in a breath, pressing her lips closed against the urge to recant, and then shook her head. "No, Mr. Spyridis. I—"

"A million."

"No!" she blurted before he offered an amount she could not refuse. "No, no, no. There's no amount that will convince me to take part in such a farce," she told him with as much conviction as she could muster.

"Two million, then."

It was a dizzying sum and Laura's stomach knotted with the desire to accept his offer. "No. I am not Lana and pretending that I am is a lie. I won't do it, no matter how much you offer. My sister has died. To pretend otherwise, even for a minute, is wrong and I won't do it."

"Even it harms no one and improves things for others?" he asked, the sound of his voice like a narcotic, deep and utterly disquieting.

"No," she said as she crossed her arms. "Lies always bring harm to someone, no matter how innocuous they may appear on the surface."

"You know this from experience?" he asked silkily.

"My experience is immaterial," she told him with a firmness she didn't feel. "What matters is that I will not pretend to be your wife."

"Because the thought of marriage to an ogre like me, even if it's only for a week, offends you?"

She blushed and diverted her attention to the smoky privacy glass between the driver and them. "I did not say that," she said in as prim a voice as she could manage. "I merely said I won't lie."

"So you don't find me offensive." His hand drifted to her shoulder and despite the multiple layers of wool and warmth, she felt his touch as keenly as if it had been on her bare skin. "We can work with that."

"Mr. Spyridis," she warned as she shifted from his touch. "I will not be manipulated into doing this. You are not my husband. You were Lana's. And my answer is no."

"You would devastate an elderly woman's final family holiday just to avoid a lie?" he countered in a velvet voice.

She cast him a suspicious glance, wary of being manipulated the way he'd manipulated any who initially protested his terse edicts. Though she'd only met him two days ago, she'd spent enough time in his company to recognize his unrelenting ambition and drive. If he wanted something, he never backed down until he'd met with success. He just kept driving forward until he'd overcome every obstacle the world saw fit to fling into his path. "What elderly woman?" she asked.

Kyros's mouth softened a bit. "My grandmother."

"Is she ill?"

"With cancer. Stage four. The doctors have given her six months, a year at the most."

Her heart cramped with empathy. She knew how hard it was to lose someone, how the denial of pending death drove a person to make crazy, irrational decisions. "I'm sorry to hear that."

"Good. Because before she dies, you and I will give her the holiday she deserves."

Laura shook her head. "No. Lies won't make things any easier for either of you. She deserves the truth from a grandson she trusts."

"No. Family means everything to *Giagiá,* and I refuse to allow Lana's untimely death to rob my grandmother of the holiday she's waited ten years to have. She believes Lana and I were blissfully wed, and I will not disabuse her of the notion now."

"Why would she believe such a lie?" Laura asked.

His nostrils flared a bit at that, but he avoided the question. "I will not bring her unnecessary grief when a mere week of your time can make her happy."

"You don't have a choice. I will not pretend to be Lana just because you're demanding it." She flicked a glance over his relaxed pose, wondering if his confidence ever wavered. "I don't care what you offer me. You won't get what you want."

His smile, as fleeting as it was sure, flashed with a hint of condescension. "I always get what I want."

"Not in this case," Laura insisted. "I cannot be bought."

"Everyone can be bought," he said as he reached to drape his arm along the back of the seat behind her shoulders. "It's just a matter of finding the right price."

She stiffened, straightening away from the glancing touch of his sleeve against the tight knot of her hair. "You're wrong," she scolded. "No amount of money will change my mind."

"Then what will?" His fingers moved to graze the collar of her brown coat, skimming the sensitive flesh of her neck.

"Nothing," she said while heat gathered in her stomach.

"Nothing?" He leaned toward her, his nearness making the breath catch in her throat. "Surely there's *something* you've always wanted but could never have."

She swallowed. Wanting impossible things was Lana's forte, not hers. She'd worked hard to be optimistic, to look for reasons to be grateful. To be happy with the life she had. "There isn't."

"You're that content?" he asked while his emerald eyes mined hers, delving for any hint of weakness, any fissure in her resolve.

Laura thought of her lonely, empty house back home, echoing with a silence and grief she'd yet to overcome. "Yes."

His thumb drifted to the tense line of her jaw. "I can give you things you can only imagine," he urged in a low, seductive voice. "Come with me for eight days and you'll never want for anything ever again."

Lifting her face from his touch, she scooted to the far

edge of the seat. "You can't give me my self-respect once it's been compromised."

He stared at her defensive posture for one lazy moment, his mouth quirking up in an indulgent, patronizing smile. "Self-respect won't pay your bills or keep your family safe."

Her throat tightened. "I have no family," she told him.

He arched a brow. "None?"

"Lana was all I had left."

The speculative gleam in his eyes sharpened. "What if I were to tell you that wasn't true?"

Every sense on alert, she tensed in readiness. "I'd think you were lying, just to get what you want."

"You have a nephew, Ms. Talbot."

She studied him in silence for several long seconds, and then shook her head. "I don't believe you." Lana had less maternal instinct than an empty designer handbag, and her patience for children had ranked with that of housecleaning and studying. "Lana would never subject herself to a pregnancy."

"Then why would I have married her?" he reasoned. "Your sister was a nobody from America, a vapid, selfish socialite who spent her days worrying about the latest fashions and the parties she might have missed. We had absolutely nothing in common beyond the child we conceived."

Laura searched his expression for evidence that he was lying to her. "You expect me to believe that Lana trapped you into marriage?"

He withdrew a picture of a black-haired infant from a pocket in his briefcase. "Titus is five months old, while Lana and I were only married for nine. You do the math."

Laura stared down at the small photo, the newborn baby's scrunched face, tiny, red and obviously still recovering from the trauma of birth. Her heart contracted with longing. He had Lana's chin. Her chin. And his name was Titus.

She had an infant nephew.

She had a *family*.

Excitement colored her voice as she asked, "When can I see him?"

"That's entirely up to you," he said without changing his inflection.

Her bubble of happiness lost some of its buoyancy. "Excuse me?"

"You can have full access the minute you agree to pose as Lana for the eight days I need."

For several seconds, Laura simply stared at Kyros, unable to believe he'd use his own child in such a manner. "You can't be serious."

"I am."

Cursing herself for revealing a vulnerability she hadn't anticipated, Laura accused, "Surely you won't deny your son a relationship with me simply because I won't pretend to be Lana."

"Why wouldn't I?" he asked.

She glared at him. "You're despicable."

"Perhaps," he said as he plucked the picture from her fingers. "But like I said, I always get what I want."

She glared at him as he tucked the photo back into his briefcase. "And I suppose it was foolish of me to hope you'd possess a core of decency."

"Oh, come now," he said, completely unmoved by her heated indictment. "I'll still pay you. Just think of all the good works you could do to offset my wickedness, or of how your involvement in Titus's life can protect him from my corruptive influence."

Without meaning to, he'd hit on yet another of her weaknesses. She never had been able to stand by while a child suffered. It was one of the reasons she'd gone into teaching. She'd wanted to care for children who might be ignored or abused at home, to create a safe haven where each student felt loved.

Kyros relaxed back against the cream leather of his seat,

his long legs splayed in apparent ease. "Say yes, and we'll fly first-class to Greece tonight. You'll have Titus in your arms by tomorrow afternoon, and enough money to buy whatever you want."

Agreeing to his conditions would be crossing a line, a line she'd refused to cross since the last time she'd impersonated her more vivacious twin. After realizing how fruitless it was to compete with Lana, she'd vowed to never live in her sister's shadow again. She'd done everything possible to separate herself from her twin, to be different. When Lana had chosen lies, Laura had chosen truth. When Lana had indulged in selfishness, Laura had focused on making others happy. Unlike her twin, Laura had lived her life outside herself, and she hadn't regretted her choices. Not once.

But she knew if she pretended to be Lana again, even if it were just for a week, she would. She'd regret trying to fit in Lana's mold.

But she'd also meet the nephew she hadn't even known she had.

She'd be able to bring love to a motherless boy.

She'd have a family again.

She'd matter.

Deep inside, her desire to belong, to be needed, urged her to succumb. To be selfish, just this once.

"I want unlimited visitation rights and full guardianship of Titus if anything ever happens to you," she whispered, her counteroffer bringing a wild rhythm to her pulse. "And the two million put in trust for him."

Kyros's relaxed posture and expression didn't alter in the slightest, but she sensed his satisfaction. "The money will go to you," he said. "I've already set up a trust for Titus."

"I don't want the money. I want access and guardianship."

"You can visit Titus anytime you wish."

"And the guardianship?"

His mouth crooked in an amused smile. "Are you expecting me to die, Laura Talbot?"

"I can hope, can't I?"

"Why would I entrust my son to you?"

"Because I will love him more than anyone else. And because I am the only maternal family he has."

"That's not the credential you'd like it to be," he said. "You are Lana's twin, after all."

"We're nothing alike," Laura told him.

Kyros's voice lowered to a purr. "Yes. I can see you like to believe that."

She felt herself color. "Do we have a deal or not?"

"Perhaps," Kyros said gravely, a glint of amusement dancing in his green eyes.

Laura skewered him with a glare. "Perhaps?"

"If I'm to make such a significant concession and risk the welfare of my son to you, there's one more condition you must meet."

"Oh?" she asked, wariness making her muscles go taut.

"You must kiss me. Whenever I deem it necessary in the coming week."

"What?" she blurted.

"If we're to convince *Giagiá* that we're happily wed, you'll need to kiss me with conviction."

"That's ridiculous! There is absolutely no reason she'd need to see us kissing!"

"You're right," he agreed easily. "But she'll expect to catch us at it nonetheless. And I must admit, I find the idea... intriguing."

Laura gaped at him in amazement, her heart thundering in her chest. "No. Absolutely not. I can't kiss you. I won't."

He shrugged. "I can assure you that it will be a pleasant experience."

"I don't care." She shook her head. "I won't kiss my sister's husband."

"The last time Lana and I kissed was the night we conceived Titus. I doubt she'd mind."

"It doesn't matter. I won't do it."

He shrugged, dismissing her claim. "Take it or leave it. The choice is yours."

Trepidation made her mouth go dry. "I'd rather negotiate guardianship than kiss you."

Kyros smiled, obviously amused by her bid to redraw the terms. "I'm sure that's the case. But I'm done bargaining. Eight days as my demonstrative wife, or there's no deal."

"But you're the one who started this whole negotiation!" she sputtered. "You can't just close it without me agreeing!"

"Can't I?"

Laura fought the trembling that claimed her limbs. "No!"

"Very well," he said. "It appears we have reached a stalemate." He didn't look remotely perturbed by the turn of events. "To which hotel shall I have my driver deliver you?"

She stared at him in mutinous silence for several seconds, realizing she'd lost her power to bargain the minute she'd expressed an interest in Titus. "Fine," she snapped. "I'll kiss you. In public only. But don't even think about curtailing my involvement with Titus."

He tipped his head, casting her a roguish smile. "I wouldn't dream of it. In fact, I can have my lawyers draw up a contract and have it ready before we even land."

"I'm revising my opinion," she grumbled. "You *are* an ogre."

"Come now," Kyros teased. "I'm not that bad."

"You are," she insisted. "You exploited your son to get what you wanted. You haven't mourned Lana's death for even one minute. And you're insisting on kissing *me,* your wife's sister. I don't know how you could get much worse."

Rather than argue, he simply extended one large, browned hand to seal the deal. "Shall we shake on it?"

Gingerly, she aligned their palms and gave their joined hands a vigorous tug.

"Your hand is freezing," he observed as his warm hand refused to release hers. His mouth hitched into a feral smile. "Are you nervous?"

"Of course I am," she told him as she tugged against his firm grip. "I'm nervous that after eight days with you, I won't know myself anymore."

His smile deepened. "Don't fret," he murmured as his thumb transcribed a small circle upon the back of her trapped hand. "I won't force you to do anything you don't want to do."

"Besides kiss you?" she snapped as she yanked her hand free of his unnerving touch.

His eyes were an emerald glitter of triumph. "Oh, you'll want to kiss me soon enough."

CHAPTER THREE

KYROS STILL simmered with the energy of victory when they settled into their first-class seats an hour later. When he'd left Greece three nights ago, he never would have anticipated Laura Talbot, his wife's *twin,* would be accompanying him home. It was a turn of events he never, even in his wildest imaginings, could have predicted.

Laura had avoided looking at him, let alone touching him, from the moment they'd shook hands to seal their deal. But he intended to change that. Soon. He'd been aroused from the moment he'd first seen her, and his fascination had only grown the longer he remained in her presence. When he'd held her delicate hand in his, he'd been nearly overcome with the desire to haul her onto his lap and have his way with her.

What was it about her that made his typical reserve vanish? It certainly wasn't her beauty—she looked enough like Lana that her appearance should have had the opposite effect. Nor could it be her vocal adherence to honesty. No twin of Lana's could possess the core of decency Laura claimed to have. No sister of his wife's could value family as much as he did.

She was just a better actress than her sister, and she'd developed weapons he hadn't had to defend against yet. Hell, she'd almost convinced *him* with her sweet, innocent and incorruptible act.

Not that he'd believed it for long. Everyone had their price and Laura wasn't *so* different from her twin in that respect. How could she be? They'd shared parents, an upbringing and a womb. He'd be a fool to forget that, no matter how much his body urged him to lower his guard around the delectable Laura Talbot.

He'd been exploited by one sister already and he wasn't about to subject himself to a second round of the same. This time, *he'd* be the one to do the exploiting. *Giagiá* deserved the family holiday only he and Laura could give her, and he couldn't allow Laura to think she could claim the upper hand in this. Yes, he'd bullied her a bit, but she *wanted* to be here now. He could sense it. He wouldn't be surprised if she begged to stay on once the holidays were over. Oh, she'd use Titus as her convenient excuse, but he'd know the real reason. Just like Lana, she'd want more of his money.

Of course, he'd make her earn every penny of it.

He slanted a glance at her and fought a smile at the way she leaned as far from him as their adjacent seats would allow, her entire body tense. Did she honestly believe he bought her innocent act? Probably. Just like Lana, she didn't know when to cut her losses and admit defeat.

But unlike her twin, Laura possessed an arsenal of weapons Lana would have never dreamed of using. Where Lana had used her beauty and her sexuality to lure men in, Laura posed as a sweet, sheltered and unsophisticated ingénue to accomplish the same ends. The combination was so damn erotic he wanted to kiss her *now,* just to see what ploy she'd try next.

She offered him a challenge he hadn't encountered before. It energized him. Intrigued him. It made him want to strip away her walls of prim disdain, just to see what sort of person was hiding beneath.

That was the real reason he'd pressed for the kissing codicil to their bargain. He wanted her scrambling to keep her

footing in this game of theirs. He wanted her disconcerted and on edge. He wanted her disoriented enough that she let her defenses slip. And if kissing were the prelude required to getting beneath her masquerade, he'd damn well make sure it happened.

Because she *was* hiding something. He could feel it. He recognized her mask because he, too, had spent a lifetime hiding the person who lurked beneath his skin.

Ever since Kyros had learned the circumstances of his birth, he'd been aware of a nagging, unending drive to prove himself worthy of the sacrifices his grandparents had made for him. He was consumed with the drive to make up for the pain his existence had brought to *Giagiá*'s life, and it compelled him to work harder and longer than anyone else, just so he could look himself in the eye without disgust. But it was never enough. There was always more he could do, more he could learn and negotiate and earn. He'd lived his life in an effort to become the man *Giagiá* had raised him to be, to make her proud. But the satisfaction of doing so remained perpetually out of reach.

Somehow, with Laura Talbot, reaching his goals felt attainable. Maybe not permanently, but for the eight days she'd be at his side, his role of perfect grandson was fully within his grasp. For the first time he could remember, he felt almost... hopeful. It was an emotion whose appeal he couldn't deny.

It was an emotion he wanted more of, no matter how much Laura resisted.

Ten hours of luxurious travel later, Laura struggled to catch her breath while Kyros led her up the imposing stretch of steps leading to his modern architectural estate. Her heart thundered within her chest as she scanned the wide, tiled terraces and offset levels of white-stucco-and-black, wrought-iron trim. The house looked like a fortress, its gardens and grounds filling two city blocks. The property was accessible

only through a tall gate, and its surrounding walls of white made her feel isolated despite its location in the heavily populated city of Athens.

What have I done?

Shivering in the bright winter sunlight, she stopped to rub her arms and gather her courage.

"What is it?" Kyros asked.

"I can't do this," she whispered as she stared up at the white mansion that had been Lana's home. How could she have been so naive to think she could pull this off? How could she have been so stupid as to allow Kyros to talk her into such a crazy ruse? "I'm sorry, but I can't."

"You can." His fingers at her back urged her forward, brooking no opposition.

She shook her head, nervous trepidation knotting her gut into a tangle of resistance. Despite the comfortable accommodations of their flight, Laura hadn't been able to relax. Premonitions of disaster had circled wildly, while all the things that could go wrong kept vying for dominance in her thoughts.

Yes, she and Lana shared identical faces, but it was Lana who had possessed the vibrant style suitable for the social whirl of a billionaire's spouse. It was Lana who'd turned heads from the time she could wave her little fists and blink her black lashes. With her flirtatious smiles and unbridled confidence, Lana had made every female within shouting distance feel awkward and ungainly by comparison.

It was a feeling Laura had grown up with, and she didn't relish the thought of taking up residence in her vivacious sister's shadow again. "I'm a horrible actress," she insisted as she stopped at the base of the entry steps. "Everyone will know I'm not Lana."

"They won't."

"You don't understand," she said, as she cast a nervous

glance at the house looming before them. "Anyone who knew Lana will realize I'm an imposter."

"I didn't," he reminded her.

"Yes. But that's because you saw me out of context. And you had no idea I even existed."

"Neither will anyone here." He tipped her chin and forced her to look at him. "Nobody here knew Lana. They didn't want to. After I lost two of my best staff because of how she treated them, the rest did their best to stay off her radar. Most of them don't speak English, and they've exchanged less than two words with her since Titus was born."

"And that's supposed to reassure me?" she cried while nervousness clawed at her throat.

His eyes searched hers. "If they suspect anything, which they won't, they'll be too grateful for their good fortune to say anything about it."

Laura bit her lip, her trepidation mounting as more rebuttals rose to the surface. "I don't even know where things are in your house," she reminded him. "They'll only have to watch me for five minutes to realize I'm a fraud!"

"You'll be fine." Kyros reached for her hand, and her fingers tingled at the heated shock of contact. "Just stick close to me and I'll ensure you don't get lost."

Too nervous to reply, Laura's heartbeat accelerated as Kyros tucked her hand into the crook of his arm and the heat of his lean body drew perilously close.

"Trust me," he said silkily. "You'll be fine. I promise. And meeting Titus will make the entire ruse worth it. Right?"

She stared at him for a suspended second, then dropped her gaze and nodded once. He took advantage of her capitulation and escorted her the rest up to his home. The giant wooden door, sleek and espresso-colored, swung soundlessly inward as they stepped over the threshold and into the quiet house. A gray-haired man rushed forward to meet them, his footsteps echoing in the cavernous foyer.

"Welcome home, Mr. Spyridis." The butler scurried to close the door behind them. "I trust your trip was satisfactory?"

"Quite," answered Kyros as he inched Laura forward.

"And yours, Mrs. Spyridis?"

"It was lovely," Laura murmured with a quivering smile. "Thank you."

The servant's thick white brows rose at that, and she realized too late that she'd been polite when Lana wouldn't have been.

"Have Lana's and Titus's suitcases been packed as I instructed?" Kyros asked.

The man stole another glance at Laura. "Yes, sir."

"Excellent." Kyros checked his watch. "Alert Miles that we will depart at five."

"Yes, sir."

Kyros shifted his attention to Laura, his bright jade gaze penetrating hers. "Shall we?" he asked as he propelled her toward the curved double staircase ahead of them.

Aware that the butler was staring at her, Laura was careful to display none of her awe at the entryway's sweeping expanse of white marble tile, vaulted ceilings and panoramic windows. Instead, she adjusted her stride to Kyros's longer one as they ascended to the second floor.

"That's right," he murmured as they turned west and headed down a hallway she assumed led to the family quarters. "Keep your chin up and your eyes straight ahead. Look haughty and unimpressed and no one will know the difference."

A trio of long windows at the west end of the hall offered a sunlit view of the city beyond the property walls, and Laura slowed to steal a glimpse of its picture-postcard views.

"Oh, my," she said under her breath. "You can see the Acropolis from here."

"Don't gawk," he answered, as if views of such historical

significance were a mundane, everyday occurrence. "You'll give yourself away."

She felt the play of muscle beneath the warm wool of his suit sleeve as he tugged her back into motion. "I didn't realize how beautiful it would be."

Her words seemed to bring him pause, because his footsteps slowed as he looked at her. "Haven't you ever been to Greece before?"

"I've never had the time or money for travel." It was yet another way she was different from Lana.

"Well, you'll have money now," he reminded her. "Enough to go anywhere."

It was a heady thought, and one that brought a flurry of guilt. She shouldn't profit from her sister's ill fortune, no matter the circumstances. "I don't want your money," she reminded him. "I only want a relationship with Titus."

He made an unconvinced sound deep in his throat and then ushered her farther down the west hallway.

"This is your room," he told her as they drew close to a dark wood set of double doors. "I'll leave you to freshen up."

"I want to meet Titus first."

"You'll meet him soon enough," he promised. "Right now, you need to ensure you have everything you'll need."

"I already have everything I need. And I want to meet Titus."

"He's with his nanny."

"Where?"

He smiled down at her. "In his rooms, five doors down."

She strode toward Titus's rooms, counting doors until Kyros's hand at her elbow stalled her progress. "You're a persistent little thing, aren't you?"

"My nephew is the only reason I'm here," she reminded him.

"Of course he is," he said as he guided her back to her

suite. "But transfer your things first, and then we'll fetch Titus. Together."

"I don't need to transfer anything," she protested.

"Yes, you do. Lana would have never deigned to carry that hideous bag you call a suitcase."

Embarrassment singed her cheeks. "There's nothing wrong with—"

"Of course there's not," he agreed with a murmur. "But this is about imitating Lana, and you need to do everything possible to behave the way she would behave for these eight days."

"I—"

"Humor me," he interrupted. "And while you're at it, you might consider changing."

"Changing?" she asked, a flare of offense bringing heat to her face. "Into what?"

"Something a little more…festive," he said, his gaze flicking down her body and then back to her face. "It *is* Christmas, you know."

"I don't have anything festive. I packed for a funeral. Not a party."

What he read in her expression must have concerned him because he ran his hands down her arms in a subtly soothing gesture. "Of course you did. Which is why I took the liberty of ordering some new things for you. They're packed for you in the suitcases you'll find in your room."

"But I didn't want you to—"

"You'll have to dress the part, whether you wish it or not." He pressed a hand against her waist and then directed her into the richly appointed suite. "So take some time to make the transformation. Shower, change and arrange your belongings. I'll be back for you soon." He checked his watch. "Shall we say at four o'clock?"

"Where are you going?"

A small smile tugged at his mouth, his eyes smoldering as his gaze dipped to her mouth. "Would you prefer that I stay?"

She gasped, the import of his words winnowing through her in a hot rush. "Of course not! I didn't—!"

"I know," he said, cutting her off with a low laugh. "I'll be in my room. Packing."

When she answered with a mutinous glare, he offered her an encouraging smile and dragged a finger along her jaw to the center of her chin. "Breathe, *glykiá mou*," he said as he tapped her lower lip with his finger. "Day one is almost over."

She sucked in a breath and stiffened, unable to relax even when he closed the door between them. Alone, and scared to death by her body's reaction to his teasing, she sank against the door and pressed a calming hand to her pounding heart.

After her breathing calmed, she straightened to observe her surroundings. Just like Lana, the rooms were overdone to the point of garishness, awash in rich shades of red, gold and espresso. It felt as if Lana had tried to cram every token of wealth into the ostentatious space, crowding every corner with priceless antiques, original artwork and heavy, gilt furniture. But along the west wall, a wide bank of windows overlooking the city made up for the jumble of expensive possessions within.

Laura escaped to the windows, shoved the filmy curtains aside and then found a glass door that opened out onto a narrow balcony. Stepping out into the cold, salt-scented air, Laura tipped her face and inhaled deeply. The brisk breeze lifted the hair off her forehead, kissed her skin with a hint of winter sun and gentled the nervousness screaming along her veins.

She could do this. She could pretend to be Lana for a handful of strangers. And in return, she'd meet the infant boy her sister had brought into the world. She'd give her nephew the love he deserved and become part of a family again.

Several minutes of deep breathing later, she returned to

the room to find her own sorry suitcase had been delivered, lined up next to the six giant pieces of white luggage at the foot of Lana's bed. To her consternation, she found that each white suitcase had been filled with an entire wardrobe of brand-new clothing, shoes and accessories whose price tags made her gasp in shock.

You'll have to dress the part.

Remembering that Lana had never met Kyros's grandmother before, Laura decided to defy Kyros's edict. She would insist her public persona and private persona were nothing alike and that in truth, she was actually quite subdued. She'd be herself, rather than her sister, and she'd get through these holidays on her own terms.

Kyros won't like it.

I don't care.

Kyros didn't deserve to get everything he wanted just because he had more money than God. He didn't deserve to have his way by using his son as a bargaining chip.

So she rearranged the contents of one of the white suitcases, trading out the outrageous, fashionable attire to make room for her own clothing. After a quick shower where she washed the grime of travel from her skin, she selected the most professional, *festive* outfit she'd brought: a navy silk outfit with a pencil skirt and a fitted jacket that she'd worn for her opening-day teacher meetings the past few years. It was dressy, more expensive than anything else she owned, and imminently suitable for a subdued Christmas celebration.

Deciding to retain her usual French twist, she repaired her hair and smoothed the stray strands back away from her face. After a quick application of lip gloss and mascara, she realized she was ready nearly twenty minutes early.

Deciding to use the extra time to meet Titus without Kyros looking over her shoulder, she cracked open her door and peered out into the wide hallway. Thankfully, it was empty, so she moved along the plush blue-and-gold carpet, counting

doors as she approached Titus's nursery. Five doors down, she drew to a halt before her nephew's room.

Would Lana knock in such a situation? Was the door shut because Titus was napping before they left for their trip? She didn't know. But given the fact that she was supposed to be his mother, she figured her arrival wouldn't be *too* suspect.

Quietly, so as not to disturb Titus in case he slept, Laura opened the door and tiptoed inside the spacious room. Slanting afternoon sunlight cast the room in warm tones of yellow and gold, casting shadows on the carpeted floor, two tidily arranged suitcases and polished white wainscoting. A quick scan of the empty crib and playpen showed that Titus wasn't asleep, while off to the left, another closed door with slivers of light around its seams drew Laura's attention. Suspecting that the nursery was a suite as well, Laura assumed the door led to an attached bathroom.

Eager to meet Titus and now confident that the baby was awake, Laura opened the door without preamble and stepped into the humid expanse of porcelain and tile. A beautiful baby with a mop of damp, black curls, his wet torso ringed by some sort of bath-seat contraption, reacted to her entry with a wide, gummy smile. He slapped at the water, kicked both legs and squealed.

"Is that you, Mr. Spyridis?" asked a portly, black-haired woman who knelt at the tub. She turned and then started, her expression rife with surprise as she saw Laura. "Oh," she stammered as the water sloshed over the rim of the tub. "I didn't expect you."

"I didn't mean to startle you," Laura said with a warm smile. "I just thought I'd check on Titus before we leave."

"You thought—" She cut herself off and blushed. "Of course. We're almost done with his bath and then I'll get him dressed for the trip. I'll have him ready in five minutes."

"I can do it," Laura said, sinking to her knees beside the

nanny. Titus reached for her with both chubby hands, dampening the front of her jacket.

"Oh, no!" the nanny said, reaching for Titus's hands. "I'm so sorry, Mrs. Spyridis, you're all wet and—"

"It's just a little water," Laura answered as she lifted the dripping baby from the tub and then wrapped him in a fluffy white towel. Looking down at his adorable face, she couldn't stop her smile. "And there's nothing wrong with a little water, is there, sweet pea?"

The nanny stared at her as if she'd sprouted the head of a Hydra before she shook herself out of her stupor and flashed a strained smile. "I'll fetch his clothing."

"Thank you," Laura said as she trailed the nanny back into Titus's room.

Within five minutes, Laura had dressed Titus in a miniature green-and-white jumper and sent the nanny to fetch a warm bottle. Alone with him now, Laura tipped the infant in her arms until she could see his face. His plump, wriggling body squirmed while his tiny, star-shaped hands reached for her chin. She smiled down at him, at the wide green eyes filled with innocent curiosity.

A cramp of longing tightened hard within her chest, swamping her with an unexpected rush of love for the child she hadn't even known existed until twenty-four hours ago. He was beautiful. Everything a mother could want in a child. Helpless to resist, she bent to kiss his forehead, inhaling the scent of baby shampoo and innocence. He was so warm. So incredibly soft and sweet.

How could Lana have abandoned such a precious little baby? She pulled Titus to her shoulder and pressed her cheek against his damp head, praising the fates for granting her entry into his life. And with the praise came the realization that mere visitation rights would never be enough.

Titus was a part of her. Whether she'd given birth to him or not was irrelevant. Whether he'd been conceived with

love or not, Titus deserved to be cherished and loved and adored for the child he was, rather than for what he could bring to the bargaining table. And Laura intended to ensure he felt all three.

She'd just have to stay out of Kyros's way and keep her head down while she did it.

Fortunately, she was good at that.

CHAPTER FOUR

KYROS PREPARED for his annual holiday visit to *Giagiá*'s, gathering his clothing and toiletries with the same economy of motion that allowed him to multitask in virtually every arena of his life. He listened to his messages as he shrugged into a fresh shirt and tie, waiting to hear the latest reports from his Chinese offices while he tucked his tuxedo and a second pair of shoes into his garment bag.

A cursory glance at his closet told him he'd left nothing behind, and so he bent to zip his packed suitcase. As he straightened, he wondered if Laura had finished packing, and which holiday outfit she'd selected. The thought of her slim curves in something other than those shapeless suits of hers sparked a hot flame of arousal.

Theos. It had only been three days since he'd met her, but she already filled his thoughts more than any other woman he'd ever met. Even though he wasn't foolish enough to trust the trembling vulnerability of her expressions, the light, feminine scent and sounds of her called to everything that was male within him. It was the first time a rational assessment of a woman's character failed to trump his attraction. He couldn't remember when he'd been so eager to be with a woman, when the mere thought of touching her skin and tasting her mouth had him pacing with agitation.

Corralling a desire he'd never had to corral before, he

moved away from the door to shove his most pressing files into his briefcase. Determined to overcome the irrational sense of urgency his wife's twin evoked, he abandoned his suite and strode toward Titus's rooms. He'd divert his thoughts to his son, and away from the intriguing female who'd pose as his wife for seven more days.

But *Theos,* restraint did not come easily.

Kyros entered the space that smelled like powder, soap and sunlight and shifted his gaze toward the playpen with its collection of bright toys and mobiles. Expecting to see Titus on his back, his chubby arms and legs windmilling with his efforts to reach the dangling bits of primary-colored animals above, the vision that met him instead hit him like a fist to the solar plexus.

His lungs tightened as he stared at Laura holding his son, both of them completely unaware of his presence at the door. "Aren't you just a beautiful boy?" she cooed as she swayed from side to side in her sensible heels.

Too stunned to move, Kyros simply stared at the startling scene of domesticity while his son gurgled in response to Laura's nonsensical compliments. Against everything that was rational, Laura appeared to belong with his son in a way that he hadn't anticipated. Disconcerted and completely disarmed, his heart thrashed against his chest, as though he'd just sprinted a mile. Trying to gather his composure, he forced his tense muscles to relax.

Theos! You're only seeing what she wants you to see!

But it didn't feel as if the scene Laura had set for him was a lie. No. The cozy warmth of his son's nursery and Laura's presence in it held a velvety, drugging quality of *rightness* he couldn't begin to deny. And it unnerved him more than he cared to admit.

He shook his head, reminding himself that Laura shared her sister's motives, no matter how masterfully she hid them behind a superficial pretense of sweetness. As soon as he

excavated the truth from behind the facade, his body would fall in line and he'd be able to view her as the manipulative woman she was.

Hauling in a steadying breath, he steeled himself against his response to her, and walked toward the pair.

Laura looked disconcertingly at ease, her trim curves moving within a suit that was almost as shapeless as the brown one he'd ordered her to change while the rhythmic motion of her hips drew his hungry gaze. Watching her and knowing she'd defied him fired a disconcerting blend of desire and reluctant respect within him. He had to grant her points for not succumbing to the lure of fashionable clothes like her twin would have. Even so, he had to suppress the crazy urge to rip that damn blue suit from her body, yank the pins from that prim twist of dark hair and show her with his mouth and tongue and hands exactly who was in charge of this charade of theirs.

The low, throaty sound of her laugh pulled his attention from her body, clamping hard within his gut and tightening his groin. Finding that Titus had wrapped his dimpled little fist in her collar, he watched as she gently scolded his son.

"Careful, sweet pea," Lana said as she gingerly withdrew the crumpled silk from Titus's mouth and then tucked the damp collar inside her buttoned jacket. "You don't want to eat that."

His nostrils flaring, Kyros battled the desire that gripped him by the throat. He forced himself to look away from the gentle swell of Laura's breast, from the alabaster skin of her white neck. But even without looking at her, he wanted to taste her, consume her, eat at her mouth until it grew soft and malleable and responsive beneath his own.

"What are you doing in here?" he asked instead, his voice a husky rasp. He cleared his throat and moved to stand at her side. "I told you to wait for me."

She flinched, drawing Titus close against her breast as she

spun to face him. "My time with Titus is limited enough as it is. I wasn't going to postpone meeting him just because you told me to."

His arousal collided with her defensive reply, making him want to smooth the lines from her forehead and bring a smile to her soft, pink mouth. But he held himself in check, surveying the room for Demetra and finding her gone. "Yes," he said in a low voice, "but I had a good reason for wanting you to wait. If you blow your cover too soon, it will ruin everything."

Her blue eyes narrowed and an obstinate expression, as firm as it was stubborn, claimed her features. "Seeing Titus ten minutes early won't blow my cover," she told him.

"It will when everyone here knew Lana couldn't be bothered to see Titus at all."

Her lush mouth firmed and she hitched Titus higher against her shoulder. "She was his *mother.*"

"Not in any way that mattered," he told her, forcibly keeping his attention on the topic at hand. "Lana expressed no interest in her son. None. She never fed him, held him, or even visited his rooms."

Laura blinked in shock while her scent rose between them.

Realizing he stood too close, Kyros inhaled thinly and took a step back. "The fact that you're here, in his room, will tell everyone that you're an imposter."

She seemed to recover from her shock, as she firmed both her chin and her expression. "So?" she said. "You said it wouldn't matter. That your staff would count themselves lucky to have me here instead."

"That's true for everyone but his nanny," he told her. "Demetra needs to believe you are who we say you are."

"Why?"

"Because she's coming with us for the holidays," he explained. "I can't have her inadvertently revealing the truth to *Giagiá.*"

"Then don't bring her."

"What?"

Laura's hand rose to cup protectively over the back of Titus's head. "Titus deserves to be loved and held and cherished by someone who isn't *paid* to care for him. *I* can be that person for the holidays, especially since I plan to be with him the whole time anyway."

"Not possible," he said, shaking his head. "You'll have other commitments."

"Like what?" she retorted.

"Like being my wife."

She stiffened visibly. "Confine my interactions with Titus, bring a nanny to keep me away from him, and I'll confess the truth to your grandmother myself."

"Don't be so dramatic," he countered with a placating tone. "You'll be grateful Demetra's with us after a day or two. Caring for an infant full-time is not the same as playing with him whenever the mood strikes."

"Don't patronize me," she snapped.

"I'm not," he said, arching a surprised brow.

"You are. I know what it's like to care for someone all day long without respite. I know what it's like to lose sleep, to be so physically exhausted you can't see straight, and to make sacrifices to make someone you love happy and comfortable. Don't you dare imply I can't handle caring for my nephew for one measly week."

He studied her expression. Her claims did not align at all with the past he'd expected her to have. "Have you nannied an infant before?"

She flushed, obviously uncomfortable with the direction of the conversation and unwilling to share more. "Titus deserves to be cared for by parents who love him," she said with a jut of her chin. "And if he can't have that, an aunt who loves him is his next best option."

"I love my son."

She scowled and then muttered, "Could have fooled me."

Stunned, he simply stared at her. From the time he'd brokered his first deal at the age of twenty-three, no one, let alone a female no bigger than his two hands, had dared to doubt his word. It was a dizzying, arousing experience, one that made his body hum at the same time that his head fumed. "Are you questioning my love for Titus?"

She lifted one delicate shoulder. "You're the one who exploited him to facilitate a lie."

"I did what had to be done," he told her. "But no matter how you choose to spin it, Titus will not be scarred at all by my so-called exploitation. My interactions with you are entirely separate from my love for him."

"Lie to yourself all you want," she persisted, standing her ground. "We both know honor and love go hand in hand. Exploit your son now, and you'll exploit him later. You won't be able to control yourself."

He became aware of his own labored breath, of the sound of his lungs pulling hard within the cage of his ribs. The last lucid sliver of his brain observed how ridiculous it was that arguing with a woman he'd just met, with Lana's *twin,* had sent his pulse into such a hard, drumming rhythm. But rationality seemed to have no place in his body's reaction. Just being near her, watching her blue eyes flash with challenge, had turned their argument into one of the most arousing experiences of his life. "You don't know the first thing about what I can and can't control."

"Really." Her voice was flat with suspicion.

"Yes. Really."

She arched one slender dark brow, and his fingers itched to trace its elegant curve. "You can control whether you lie or not, yet you don't. You could have chosen honor and truth, but you didn't."

"Neither did you."

"Only because you blackmailed me," she challenged as she shifted Titus to her other shoulder.

"No. I didn't. I'm just a better negotiator than you and you don't like it," he shot back. "I leveraged your desire to meet Titus so *Giagiá* could get what she needs. And losing to me makes you mad. It has nothing to do with whether I love my son."

"Nobody *needs* lies," she grumbled.

He cocked his head, flicked his gaze over her torso and then lowered his voice to an intimate hum. "Yet you agreed to the lies, didn't you?"

She stiffened. "Only because you left me no choice," she argued out in a low, frustrated voice.

"You always have a choice," he told her. "And you know it. You're just upset that you failed to realize it."

Her gaze skewered his while the pink bow of her mouth firmed into a frown. "I don't like you. You're a terrible human being."

Aware that this was the most critical a woman had ever been of him, he stared at her while his body echoed to touch her, to lose himself in her until he could banish this obsession with a female he barely knew. "Fortunately, it's not necessary for you to like me," he said.

Irritation flirted with the dark line of her brows. "Good. Because I don't."

"I know. But you *are* attracted to me, and I'm willing to work with that."

"Excuse me?"

Arousal kindled anew in his groin, fired by her flushed cheeks and offended posture. "It's all right," he soothed with an insincere expression of apology. "I'm used to it."

Her mouth opened, then snapped closed while she grappled for a suitable reply.

A low laugh rumbled in his chest. "You're not going to disagree with me?"

She swallowed, then braced her shoulders, appearing for all the world as if she were girding herself for battle. "What would be the point? You'd just take it as a challenge to prove me wrong."

He offered her an unapologetic smile. "I do have a reputation to maintain."

"I'm sure you do," she said with a snide twist of her pretty little mouth.

"Tell you what," he offered. "I'll leave Demetra here. On one condition." He dragged his gaze over her shapeless navy suit, aware that even as he did so, he could hear his pulse accelerate within his ears.

"Another condition?" she said, and her breath sounded as thin as his felt.

"Yes." He dipped his focus to her mouth and lingered there for one protracted beat of time before returning. "You may not use Titus as an excuse to avoid your role as my wife. If I want you with me, you're with me whether Titus is awake or not. Understood?"

The crests of her cheeks turned crimson and her blue gaze strayed over his body in a swift, seemingly involuntary perusal. "That's not fair."

The subtle display of feminine interest fired him with an unwelcome heat and made him want to bend her backward over his arm and devour her pink mouth until she gasped out her surrender. "As you've already so eloquently pointed out, I don't play fair."

She dropped her gaze to Titus. "Fine."

Kyros watched as his son's small hand gripped the neckline of her dress, tugging the silk in a lopsided line across her throat. The sight made a coil of heat gather ground in his gut. Awash with the need to touch her, he reached for her arm and spun her toward the hallway. "Come."

A sudden jolt of heat arrowed through him when his fingers accidentally grazed the curve of her breast. Startled

by the inadvertent contact, his gaze flew to hers, only to be ensnared by the surprise he read in her wide eyes. Her quick intake of breath and the fresh flood of color turning her cheeks to flame tempted him to believe she'd been as caught off guard as he, that she'd been unable to censor her body's response before revealing itself to him. But even as the innocence of her reaction tore through him, urging him to touch her again, he knew better than to be duped by her seemingly involuntary invitation.

He released her as if he'd been stung, his thoughts too muddled for rational reasoning. "My pilot is waiting," he said in a strangely hoarse voice. He cleared his throat. Forced an impersonal tone. "Have you traveled by helicopter before?"

"No." Laura's nostrils flared and she moved Titus to her other shoulder. "Will that be a problem?"

He wanted to press his fingertip to the thrumming bit of flesh at her throat, to test the rapid, hummingbird beat of her heart. "Not at all."

"Good."

Before he had a chance to reply, she spun on her heel and stalked past him. She didn't touch him, didn't even look at him, but her scent rose between them, igniting a reaction so fierce his knees nearly buckled. It was an unfamiliar, complex scent, a drugging blend of musk and honey and heat that made his heart beat painfully against his ribs.

His skin felt too tight, his lungs too small, and he struggled to breathe normally through parted lips.

Theos. If he didn't figure out a way to control his reaction to her, and soon, he was going to go mad.

CHAPTER FIVE

LAURA HAD never seen a luxury helicopter before. She barely had time to conceal her awe before Kyros's presence at her back pressed her forward. Having confined her air travel to economy seats on the cheapest flights possible, she fought not to gape at the sleek private cabin, the quartet of huge buff-colored leather seats, the built-in bar and the curved windows overlooking the sea. She claimed one of the back chairs and covertly watched Kyros as he strapped Titus's carrier into the center-most seat and then settled in next to her.

Within minutes, they were aloft, and their stomach-tingling ascent tempted Laura to press her face against the glass to watch Kyros's estate dwindle below them, to gasp at the scenery and point out the receding beaches and the closeness of the waves. But she held herself in check, refusing to exclaim over the wonders of their swift, propellered journey.

Instead, she shifted her focus to the darling child seated across from her. Titus grinned at her, kicking his plump legs as the helicopter lifted and canted its path over the sea. She smiled back, unable to restrain her joy at sharing this stolen time with her beautiful nephew. He had to be the most good-natured child ever born, and Laura watched him until he finally tired of the novelty, rubbed his eyes and then slumped into sleep.

Wishing she, too, could escape into sleep, her gaze slid

warily toward Kyros. He was watching her with the same speculative gleam as before, as if he were trying to unravel all her secrets and gauge her reactions before she even knew how she'd react herself. The tension was a palpable weight between them, making her wonder how they were ever going to deceive his grandmother about the status of their relationship. Laura bit down on her inner cheeks, unnerved by the prospect of feigned intimacy that lay ahead.

She was *far* too attracted to him, despite the fact that she didn't like him. She could feel his heat, the warmth of his skin, and could almost hear the steady, rhythmic beat of his heart. The crisp blend of scents, of shaving cream, cologne and man, filled the luxurious interior of the helicopter. It made her afraid to breathe, to inhale any bit, however small, of the man whose bride she was pretending to be.

What if he wanted her to act the role of wife beyond the public kisses he'd threatened? What if he pulled her against the flexing muscles of his chest and urged her to explore the wide cage of his ribs and back with her bare palms? Swallowing against the impossible image, Laura dragged her gaze aside. His square hand claimed her peripheral vision, resting against his thigh, and she wondered how those long fingers might feel upon her breast, shaping her tender flesh before he bent to take her in his hot mouth—

Stop it! The frantic command roared through her brain, reminding her that the beautiful, intense man at her side would never be hers. She squeezed her eyes shut, willing her attraction into submission and reminding herself that she didn't even *want* him! He'd been Lana's husband. Her *sister's,* for God's sake! But the admonition did little to dispel her body's reaction. Her limbs were weighted with a heavy, warm ache, and her lungs labored to claim even the shallowest of breaths.

"How much longer before we arrive?" she asked in an effort to divert her thoughts.

"Why?" came his amused reply. "Are you that eager to begin your role as my besotted wife?"

He'd deliberately misinterpreted her question, rather than recognizing it for the desperate plea for distraction it was. Thank God. Having him realize the truth of her thoughts would spell disaster. Determined to quell her desire for a man she knew better than to want, she licked her dry lips. "Not at all," she said. Seizing on the first idea that popped into her head, she tipped her chin and said, "I'm just curious about your grandmother, and was hoping I'd have enough time to learn about her and what she'll expect from me."

Kyros made a low sound of doubt and then turned his laserlike focus on her. "She's a typical Greek grandmother—bossy, demonstrative and opinionated."

"Did she disapprove of you marrying an American woman?"

"She only cares that I am happy."

"And she believes you were happy with Lana?"

"I told her my bride was beautiful, an amazing mother and desperately in love with me. Why wouldn't I be?"

"You expected *Lana* to fill that role for you?" Laura cast him a wary glance. "Even she wasn't *that* good of an actress."

His smile sent an erotic shiver of awareness clear to her toes. "Then I suppose I should count myself lucky to have you here instead."

She shook her head. "I'll grant that I can care for Titus convincingly. But being desperately in love with you? I'm afraid I can't help but fail."

"That's why I insisted on you kissing me," he told her, sounding as if it were an entirely reasonable solution to his problem. "With some practice, kissing can look enough like love to convince anyone."

She shook her head and withdrew as much as the seats would allow. "I don't need practice."

He arched a brow and his gaze dipped to her mouth and

then back. "Really," he said. "You have that much experience."

A heated flush stole over her cheeks. "I have enough."

"You'll pardon my doubt. And my insistence on a rehearsal."

"No rehearsals," she said. "I only agreed to kiss you in public, when your grandmother was watching."

"Need I remind you that you also agreed to make it convincing?"

"I *will* make it convincing," she bluffed.

An uneven smile betrayed his skepticism. "Prove it."

"No."

He leaned toward her until their faces were mere inches apart, his voice turning to liquid silver as he murmured, "What are you afraid of?"

"Afraid?" she forced out on a trilling laugh while she pressed back into her seat, trying to create space between them while her hands gripped the armrests. "I'm not afraid."

He reacted to her claim with a knowing smile, the unnerving calm of his voice at odds with the simmering tension in his big body. "Maybe you should be."

"I'm not," she scoffed while her pulse clamored wildly within her ears. "Kissing is kissing." She tried to dismiss him with a haughty arch of her brow. "I'm sorry if that bruises your fragile ego, but one man is the same as another. I don't have to *practice* to prove that to you."

"You obviously haven't kissed enough men," he purred while his fingers rose to stroke the ridge of her jaw. "If you had, you'd know that kisses are like wine. Some are rich and full-bodied, some are light and sweet, and some can make you drunk before you've finished one glass," he told her while his eyes teased her with scalding, emerald intensity.

"And I suppose you'd classify your kisses as the latter?" she challenged, while the insidious pleasure of his touch spread through her in rolling, heated waves.

His fingers moved to her nape, branding her as his voice dipped dangerously low. "Of course I do. And you would to, were you brave enough to sample one."

She forced a dismissive laugh. "Flirt with me all you want. I won't change my mind," she lied. "I don't want to kiss you and I won't until your grandmother demands it."

"The downside of being honest all the time is that you never quite learn how to lie convincingly." His smile deepened as his gaze dipped to her lips. "And right now, everything but that mouth of yours is telling me you want to kiss me very much."

Her throat felt dry and her tongue felt thick and clumsy. Her vision was blurry and she couldn't seem to breathe properly. "I don't," she managed to say in a thin thread of a voice.

"Shall I call your bluff?" he whispered while his nostrils flared like that of a stallion catching the scent of his mate.

She shamelessly reveled in his reaction, knowing that now, at this very second, he saw only her. Not Lana. *Her.*

"Or shall I simply pretend to believe you and release you as you claim to want?"

"Yes," she answered faintly while her heart thrashed against her ribs, driving the breath from her chest.

"Yes what?"

"Release me," she begged, her fingers digging into the soft leather even as every cell strained toward him.

His eyes crinkled as he studied her. "I don't think so," he breathed as both hands moved to bracket her skull. She felt utterly possessed, incapable of protest, as his thumbs transcribed small, drugging circles at the corners of her mouth. "I think I'd rather call your bluff," he said in a low whisper.

Too startled to breathe, let alone push him away, she remained unmoving as his mouth slowly lowered to hers. Though he claimed her with only the barest hint of lip against lip, she felt the connection as if she were chained irrevocably to him.

Frozen in place by a firestorm of longing, she was helpless to control her untutored response. Though the kiss began gently, exquisitely soft and taunting, he seduced her into allowing him inside. His demanding mouth settled over hers, drugging her with an intimate blend of silk and heat.

Defenseless and stunned, she tasted him as the tip of his tongue teased her lips open and stroked in sultry invitation. He delved deep, molding her mouth to his and tipping her head for better access. She'd never been kissed this way. She shuddered and swayed, too unmoored to do anything but clutch at his shoulders and relent.

He took advantage of her acquiescence, reaching with both hands to haul her closer. One broad palm slid low against her spine, and before she even realized he'd moved her, he'd crushed her aching breasts up against his chest. Feeling the tension rise between them, she fought the tide of arousal that threatened to pull her under. Her hands fluttered ineffectually against the sides of his rough jaw, the hint of stubble abrading her palms.

She had to stop him. She had to stop this craziness… she had to, oh… She squirmed, a warm coil of heat making her pulse pound heavily at the apex of her thighs while her stomach fluttered with anticipation. Her legs shifted restlessly in an instinctive bid for release, and she flattened her hands against his shoulders in a futile bid to create space between them.

He growled low in his throat and bent her backward over his arm. His mouth trailed heat down the side of her neck to her collar, his tongue teasing the sensitive flesh. Searing desire warred with her conscience, and a small whimpering moan escaped her.

"Wait," she gasped as she reached for his head and dragged his marauding mouth from her flesh. "We can't… I… You have to stop."

He released her immediately, and then felt the separation

like an arctic blast. His eyes met hers with a glimmer of triumph while a humorless smile cut a lopsided curve between his lips. She stared at him, her heart in her throat, trying to calm her panting breaths.

He returned her stare with the same disconcerting blend of anger and desire she'd experienced before. It felt as if he could consume her with nothing more than a glance, as if he wanted to reach deep, deep inside, and claim her soul as his own. It frightened her how much she wanted to give it to him, how desperately she wanted to give him everything no matter the cost.

"You're right." His voice, low and dangerously soft, pebbled her skin with the poignancy of touch. "You don't need to practice."

If Kyros hadn't spent the majority of his adult life honing his legendary control, he would have succumbed to the temptation to seduce the beautiful imposter he'd hired to play his wife. He would have laid her out on his lap and had his way with her, the consequences be damned.

But he'd made the same colossal mistake with one twin; he'd be a fool to repeat his error with the other.

Despite the mounting evidence to the contrary when it came to Lana and her sister, he was *not* a fool.

He learned from his mistakes.

Theos. He *did.* Looking at her now, at her flushed skin and wide-eyed wariness that had blinded him with lust, he berated himself for not immediately recognizing her power.

Oh, she was good, he'd grant her that, but he was better. She was too responsive to him, too unprepared to grapple successfully with the attraction that had flared so unexpectedly between them. He could tell that the sexual awareness heating the close quarters of his helicopter, thickening the air and heightening her senses, had unmoored her in a way no verbal battle could have accomplished. The simmering ten-

sion between them held an unexpected force he sensed she hadn't planned on, and if he hadn't been so rattled himself, he'd have recognized the danger of exploiting it.

But he hadn't. Like an undefeated general surveying the field of his lesser enemy, he'd arrogantly plied her momentary weakness without examining the consequences of his actions. He'd acted quickly, denying her the opportunity to adapt her strategy. One look at her dilated pupils, at the agitated working of her lungs, and he'd moved in to press his advantage. Confident that he came from a position of superior strength, he'd kissed her just to prove she was in over her head. To prove she'd entered a battle she was unprepared to win. He'd plied her with one ravenous kiss, intending to call her bluff and show her that he was the one in control of her.

It had been a tactical error of staggering proportions.

To his disgust, the kiss had broadsided him as much as her. Anger and arousal battled with such ferocity that he had trouble quelling the cravings of his unruly body. He *hated* that his response to her had rendered him just as off-kilter as she. No one, least of all Lana's sister, should have the power to burrow beneath his defenses and make him *feel*.

Lana's twin sister had done what no other woman had ever done, and the realization tasted like ash in his mouth. Lana, despite all her calculated ploys, had never elicited this burning roar of desire that threatened to overwhelm him. She'd never tempted him to relinquish the upper hand. To surrender. Ever. The woman he'd married, with her rehearsed flirtations and contrived emotions, had nothing on her sister.

No. Laura, with her soft, innocent eyes and delicate blushes, was far more dangerous.

And he'd been foolish enough to betray that fact to her.

His lips thinned as he glared at the gorgeous actress who clutched the handle of his door like some startled virgin who'd just discovered the wonders of lovemaking.

No matter what she did, no matter how she played him, he would *not* allow her to gain the upper hand.

When they alighted from the helicopter, it was to the waning light of dusk, three servants who'd come to collect their luggage and a brisk winter breeze. Laura shivered, tugged her jacket around her torso and then followed Kyros from the launchpad toward the stone walkway encircling his grandmother's island estate. She tried to calm her frazzled nerves by focusing on the gentle back-and-forth motion of Titus in his carrier at Kyros's side.

But when she looked up to gain her bearings, a lurch of surprise accompanied her first up-close glimpse of their holiday destination. *This* is where Kyros's grandmother lived? From the helicopter and its aerial view, she hadn't noticed the scope and magnitude of the palatial marble estate. But now, with twilight casting its Ionic columns in faint hues of lavender and blue, she felt a panicked urge to escape.

Kyros must have sensed her unease, because he bent his dark head to hers and closed his free hand loosely around her upper arm. "You'll be fine," he reassured her tersely as they climbed the steps toward the palace's opulent entry. "Just follow my lead." And with that low command, he dropped her arm to rap against the door.

"Agapitó agóri mou!" an old woman called from an electric wheelchair as soon as the carved white door opened. With a press of the chair's controls, she glided soundlessly forward as Laura and Kyros stepped over the threshold. The woman dismissed her butler with a wave of her hand, her face creasing in a web of smile lines as she lifted her cheek for Kyros's kiss. "I thought you would never arrive!"

Kyros, one hand wrapped around his son's carrier, straightened. *"Giagiá,"* he said warmly. "You look as beautiful as always."

"I look like death, and you know it," she said with a dis-

missive flutter of her fingers before she leaned to peer inside
the baby carrier. "Oh, Kyros!" she gasped as she pressed her
hand to her narrow chest. "What a beautiful Christmas gift
you have brought to me!"

It was clear to Laura that Kyros's grandmother had been
stunning in her youth, as her classic bone structure remained
despite her age and failing health. Her hair, undoubtedly
once as thick and black as Kyros's, was now thin and gray,
visibly ravaged by cancer treatments. But her eyes were the
same pale green as her grandson's, and she still managed to
look beautifully elegant in her gray cashmere sweater and
slim black pants.

"We named him Titus," Kyros told her. "After *Pappoús.*"

"Of course you did," his grandmother murmured with a
pleased hum. She ran a frail hand over Titus's unruly black
curls, and grinned before looking back at her grandson's face.
"He looks exactly like you did at this age."

"There's definitely no doubt as to who his father is," he
answered with a hint of self-deprecating humor in his voice.

His grandmother, her face lined with pride, caught sight of
Laura behind Kyros's wide back. With a thin gasp of delight,
she waved Laura forward with a flutter of her spidery hand.
"Forgive me for not noticing you sooner!" she said, leaning
to clasp Laura's fingers. "You must be Kyros's lovely young
bride and Titus's mother, yes?"

"I am," she lied. Laura returned the welcoming squeeze,
noticing how insubstantial the old woman's fingers felt between hers. Kyros's grandmother reminded Laura of a waning autumn day before the first fall of snow: wispy, frail and
smelling of cloves and gingerbread. She looked like the faint-
est puff of air might blow her away, and Laura wondered how
long she'd been ill. "Kyros has told me so much about you,
and I can see that he has not exaggerated at all." She paused,
not sure what she was supposed to know or how she should
proceed, when Kyros interrupted.

"One doesn't dare exaggerate about *Giagiá*," Kyros said with a smile. He looped an arm low against Laura's waist and then gazed down at her face with a look of raw adoration so dangerously genuine, it stole her breath. "Lana, this is Iona, my grandmother. *Giagiá,* this is Lana. My heart, my wife, and the devoted mother of my son."

He returned his attention to his grandmother while Laura fought off dizziness. How was she supposed to carry on a normal conversation with Kyros waxing on about the multiple roles she was expected to play?

"Lana. What a lovely name." Iona surveyed Laura with her light green eyes, her warmth and intelligence gleaming from their clear depths. "I understand you are American?"

Trying to ignore Kyros's disturbing presence at her side while grappling with a script she hadn't had time to prepare, Laura managed a friendly, if somewhat unsteady, smile. "Yes, ma'am. I was born near the northwestern coast. In a small Oregon town called Green Pines."

"Ah. Oregon. I've heard of it," she said while her grandson's fingertips drifted lower to press against the ridge of Laura's right hip. "It is quite green there, is it not?"

Stiff with tension, Laura forced herself to concentrate on the welcoming visage of her hostess. "Very much so."

Iona tipped her head, as curious and wobbly as a newborn bird's. "How did a girl from Oregon end up here in Greece?"

Determined to integrate as much truth into her deception as possible, Laura answered, "I've always wanted to travel, for as long as I can remember."

"To Greece in particular?"

She answered with a small shake of her head. "I wanted to go everywhere, though Greece definitely topped the list." Her smile wavered, her brain still wrestling with the stark contrast between the surreal situation she'd found herself in and the romantic dreams of her childhood. "I was forever planning my fantasy escape."

"Escape?" Iona asked with a curious arch of her silver brows. "Did you need to escape your home, dear?"

"Oh, no! Not at all!" Laura rushed to clarify. "I love Oregon! It's just nice to experience a place with so much sun and sea and beautiful color."

Satisfied, Iona nodded. "Not to mention handsome men," she added with a significant glance at her grandson.

Remembering the heated kiss she'd shared with Kyros, Laura felt her cheeks flood with color. She ducked her head, excruciatingly aware of his thigh pressed so close to hers. "That, too."

"Oh, would you look at that! I have not seen such a pretty blush for years," Iona observed before addressing Kyros. "No wonder you are smitten. She is exquisite."

Uncomfortable with the compliment, Laura murmured, "I prefer to think of myself as ordinary."

"Ordinary?" Iona repeated, while Laura felt Kyros's hot regard shift to her. "I think not."

"I'm with *Giagiá* on this," Kyros said. Emerald eyes caressed her with a warmth she'd not anticipated, sending a current of desire humming along her veins. "You steal my breath away, *glykiá.*"

"Th-thank you," Lana managed to respond, while her smile trembled against her cheek.

"You're welcome," he murmured.

His grandmother watched the two of them, her perceptive green eyes narrowing as she studied her grandson's absorbed expression. "If I did not know Kyros as I do," she observed, "I would wager you blinded him with your beauty."

"If Kyros was shallow enough to be blinded by beauty," Laura answered, trying to shift away from his unnerving touch with an unsteady laugh, "I would never have married him."

"Lucky for me, I get both beauty and brains, don't I, *agápi*

mou?" Kyros held her fast and grinned down at her, a disarming, charming flash of white against dark.

"My grandson is no fool," Iona added. "He would not have married you if you did not have the character to match your outward beauty."

"Thank you," she said, while a beat of panic thrummed low in her belly. It was *she* who was the fool, thinking she had any chance of continuing this crazy ruse without Iona discerning her lies. It was only a matter of time before Iona figured out she was not the woman her grandson had married.

"Come." Iona activated her wheelchair again, turning toward the center of the house and rolling across the polished white marble of the foyer. "I will show you to your rooms so you can dress for dinner." She angled a look over her shoulder at Kyros. "The gold suite in the east wing is suitable, is it not?"

"The gold suite is perfect," Kyros answered as he trailed behind them.

This is insane, Laura thought as she swallowed back the knot of trepidation lodged in her throat. What had Kyros been thinking, to believe for a second that she could pull this off?

You'll be fine, Kyros had assured her as they'd approached the island estate. *Just follow my lead.* He'd probably suspected that she'd want to renege, that lying went against her nature. Yet he'd also divined that the thought of spending time with Titus, the prospect of feeling like a mother despite the deception of the role, would be too big a temptation to resist.

Hopefully, Kyros hadn't divined that she was drawn to *him* as well.

CHAPTER SIX

WATCHING *GIAGIÁ,* with her bony hands, white curls and nearly translucent skin, Kyros felt a surge of pending loss he didn't want to face. But face it, he must. He knew this was his last chance to provide *Giagiá* the holiday happiness she deserved. She looked healthier than the last time he'd seen her, but he also knew it was just a matter of time before things got worse.

When she'd refused to undergo further treatment, claiming that she wanted the end of her life to be spent at home, his arguments had fallen on deaf ears. She'd wanted her last months to be free of pain, free of needles and procedures and drugs that made her feel worse than the cancer did. And though it had killed him to relent, he'd accepted her decision. He'd arranged for her to have the best palliative care, the best nurses and doctors available. He'd allowed her to stay in her home despite his wish that she move to the city with him.

Even so, he felt a pang of frustration as he followed *Giagiá* into the gold suite. How could he take care of her when she refused to leave the island?

The room looked just as he'd remembered: large and rectangular, with opulent decor grand enough for visiting royalty. Wall sconces cast a warm amber glow over the giant four-poster bed, its covers drawn down at a diagonal and its canopy adorned with swags of gold, cream and white.

An overstuffed white couch, a pair of matching curved

armchairs and a small table created a conversation nook before a large, unlit fireplace along the west wall. To the east, large, floor-to-ceiling windows promised a breathtaking view of the morning sunrise.

Even though Kyros had owned the estate for eight years, having free and ready access to the rooms he'd been barred from as a child was a mental adjustment every time he visited. He supposed he should be used to it by now, but he wasn't. He still felt like the same bastard grandchild of a servant he'd always been.

"I've had the adjacent suite set up for Titus," *Giagiá* said as she gestured toward the adjoining room visible at the south corner. She rolled to the connecting door that had been left open in welcome and then reached back to pat Titus in his baby carrier. "Look, Titus," she said, pointing toward the freshly painted suite. "There's a new crib, a bassinet and a rocking chair, just for you."

"Thank you," Kyros said as he reached to clasp his grandmother's narrow shoulder. "I'm sure we'll all be very comfortable."

His grandmother beamed up at him as she turned back to survey their room. Exhaling in satisfaction, she rolled back toward the hallway. "Excellent," she said. "I will let Helen know you are here. Christmas dinner will be served as soon as you are ready." She then closed the door behind her, plunging the room into silence.

Kyros turned back to watch as Laura stepped from marble tile to rug, the clicking sound of her heels immediately muffled by the plush white wool inlaid with gold Byzantine crosses. Against all reason, his chest tightened while a thrumming pulse of pleasure and gratitude gathered in his veins.

So far, she hadn't made a single mistake. She'd played the role of nervous, biddable wife to perfection. Even now, she reminded him of a little bird, her tidy hands fluttering about

her waist and her eyes round with wonder as she turned to survey their decadent room with its big, white bed.

"You don't expect me to share that bed with you, do you?" she asked, her gaze darting to the giant mattress with its artfully arranged covers.

Watching her, he was struck anew at his body's leaping response to her nearness. She looked like a scared wraith, left behind by a tribe of mischievous fairies. If he were foolish enough to believe the display, he would have heeded the urge to comfort her. To touch her and smooth the worry from her pleated brow. But she was a risk he didn't dare take until he figured out her game. Until he figured out what she was hiding, she was off-limits.

"Because I'm telling you right now, I won't. I did not agree to continue this ruse behind closed doors."

"I'm aware of that."

"Good."

"Which is why I'll be sleeping on the couch."

"In here?" she squeaked.

He walked toward her, his footsteps muffled by the thick carpet, and stopped mere inches from her stiff little body. Her hair, a shining blend of espresso and mahogany, remained in its tidy knot, just begging to be messed up. He wanted to release its pins and explore its length with his fingers. He wanted to draw her close enough that he could catch her scent. But he resisted. For now. "*Giagiá* needs to believe we're a happily married couple. Requesting separate rooms might make her suspicious, don't you think?"

Her face blanched as her gaze skipped from the bed to the floor to his chest.

"I won't touch you," he told her softly. "I promise." *Not yet, at least.*

"Somehow, that doesn't reassure me very much," she answered, and he smiled.

"I imagine it doesn't." He clasped his hands behind his

back in order to suppress the urge to kiss her again. If nothing else, their kiss in the helicopter had shown him that she was dangerous. When he'd compared kisses to wine, he'd never expected *hers* to be the finest he'd ever sampled. And much as he yearned for another taste, he knew better than to court the madness such an error would bring. He would dabble with her, slake a lust that had gone too long denied. But not yet. Not until he knew he could control himself and his reaction to her. "But I can assure you. No matter what Lana might have told you about me, I *am* capable of controlling my baser urges."

The fact that he might require control where she was concerned seemed to perturb her, as a pink blush climbed from her throat to her cheeks. "Lana didn't tell me anything about you," she said in a strained voice.

"She didn't?" he asked, trying to decide whether to be offended or relieved.

"She only contacted me once in the past ten years."

"Really?" he asked, undecided as to whether he believed her or not.

One narrow shoulder hitched while her eyes avoided his. "Lana didn't much care for Momma or me," she admitted in a small voice. "She thought our small-town ways were boring and uptight."

He fought a smile. "You?" he teased. "Uptight?"

The pink that tinted the crests of her cheeks darkened to red. "Lana was always much wilder than I was, and she didn't like it when I tried to be her voice of reason. She couldn't wait to leave me behind along with everything else she hated about her life."

Which would explain why the twins' skills for seduction were so different. "I guess that's the reason I didn't know about you."

She nodded glumly, her sad little mouth drooping into a curve he wanted to test with his finger. "She liked to pretend

that her past was much more interesting than it really was. We didn't even know where she was until she showed up in the tabloids with you."

"Then I imagine you've already grieved her passing, having not seen her in so long."

Laura's gaze lifted to his, her eyes flooded with guilt. "Is that horrible of me?"

"No," he admitted, wondering about this new angle to her game. "It's honest."

"It makes me feel like a terrible sister."

"Don't," he corrected. "It was she who cut the ties with you. Not the other way around."

She winced. "Still, though. If I'd tried harder, if I'd forced her to talk to me, maybe she wouldn't have made such reckless choices. Maybe I could have convinced her to change."

"Glykiá mou," he said. "If *I* couldn't keep her in line, no one could."

Visibly surprised, she looked up at him with her curious blue eyes. "Did you try?"

"Of course. We were married. She was the mother of my son."

"Then why was she in New York instead of home with you?"

A scowl pulled at his brow. He did *not* like being reminded of Lana's defection. "Lana left Greece because she was bored. With marriage, with motherhood, with anything that required her to attend to things outside of herself."

"We shouldn't speak ill of the dead," she reminded him in a soft voice.

"You're right. I'm sorry," he said dryly. "I forget that I'm supposed to be the grieving widower."

"You didn't have to marry her just because she was pregnant, you know. Women raise children on their own all the time."

He exhaled noisily, uncomfortable with the direction of

their conversation. "Yes. But I know what it's like growing up without a father. I refused to do that to my own child."

Laura stared at him in shock. "You grew up without your father?"

"Yes."

"What happened?"

"What always happens when a dishonorable man seduces an innocent girl," he said. "He abandoned her the day he learned she was pregnant."

"Oh." Her features softened while her small hand pressed against her chest. "That must have been horrible for your mother."

"It was. It killed her will to live," he said in a flat voice. "She died the day I was born."

"I'm sorry."

For some reason, the sympathy he read in her eyes angered him. "Don't be. It was a long time ago."

"Have you ever met him?"

"No. But he tried to establish contact once I'd made my first million." His smile felt like it had been carved from stone. "I found I wasn't much interested in building a relationship with him."

She nodded as she studied his face, no trace of judgment in her clear blue eyes. "I'm surprised you risked a pregnancy with Lana, given your history."

The truth was, he'd made a mistake. A mistake he couldn't fix. A mistake he'd never make again. "It wasn't intentional, I can assure you."

"I believe you," she said quietly. "Very few men were capable of making wise choices when it came to Lana."

What about when it comes to you? "I was celebrating a merger I'd worked all year to complete, and lacking my typical defenses against a beautiful, willing woman." His jaw flexed, the details of that night still frustratingly out of reach. "And the irony of it is, I *never* forget protection. *Ever.*"

She swallowed and again dropped her gaze, as if talk of conception embarrassed her. "But you have Titus now," she reminded him, "so it wasn't all bad."

"No. It wasn't." He stared at the top of Laura's head, wondering how much more of the truth to share. *What the hell,* he thought. Lana didn't deserve his discretion. "Though I could have made things easier for myself."

Her head lifted at that.

He felt his muscles tense, remembering Lana's initial proposal. "I could have merely bought Titus from Lana. It was what she would have preferred."

Laura gaped at him. "Lana tried to *sell* Titus to you?" she clarified on a stunned whisper.

He nodded, begrudgingly impressed by how authentic her reaction seemed to be. "For five million dollars. She had the papers all drawn up, ready to sign, and promised I'd never have to see her again if I agreed."

Laura shook her head, apparently at a loss for words. "I... no wonder you don't... Wow."

"Yes. Wow," he agreed. "Unfortunately for Lana, I don't like to leave a trail of bastards in my wake, nor do I get women pregnant and then pay them off to keep it a secret."

"I'm sorry she—"

"It's not your fault," he interrupted. "Lana made her choices and I made mine. All we can do is move forward and hope that things improve."

"I just never realized that she'd..."

"Yes. I'm sure you didn't. But I learned from the experience. And I suspect you'll do a much better job playing my contented, loving wife than Lana would have."

Her eyes, troubled as a storm at sea, tracked his expression. "Your grandmother is a lovely woman and I will do my best to make her happy. You don't need to worry."

"I know," he said. Laura had the sweetness act down to a

science, and *Giagiá* was too trusting to ever doubt her performance.

She pressed her mouth into a firm line and nodded. "Neither Titus nor your grandmother deserves to be wounded by Lana's selfishness."

"No. They don't."

"Nor did you."

Surprised, Kyros looked down at her face until she blushed and averted her gaze.

Visibly discomfited, she moved to collect the largest of her suitcases and then rolled it to the walk-in closet to unpack. He'd have helped her, but he sensed that unnecessary closeness would be unwise for both of them. He still hadn't figured out how to deal with her, and he didn't wish to upset the tentative balance they'd reached.

So instead, he sat on the couch and watched as she retrieved a week's worth of clothing, all of it in shades of brown, navy, charcoal and taupe. He suppressed a smile, realizing she'd exchanged the clothing he'd ordered for her own subdued, shapeless wardrobe. She displayed a commitment to her role he'd thought new clothing would undermine. Again, he found himself reluctantly impressed by a woman he would have preferred to dislike.

"What do you do for a living?" he asked, wondering what career would require such a somber selection of suits.

"I'm a teacher," she told him. Her hands, slender and oddly erotic, threaded hangers through a collection of suits, pants and sweater sets. "At least, I was. For the past few years, I've only been able to take the occasional substitute teaching position."

"Why?"

She stared at him for a long moment, as if debating whether to answer him. "My mother had a severe stroke three years ago, and another shortly thereafter. Her therapies

were pretty involved and time-consuming, so I had to give up my contract to care for her."

No wonder she'd been so offended when he'd implied she couldn't care for Titus properly. "Is she recovered now?"

Her shoulders stiffened and her hands tightened around a brown turtleneck, crushing it against the wooden hanger. "She died six months ago."

That would explain the shadows of grief he'd read in her expression whenever she let down her guard. Not only had she lost her estranged sister but she'd lost her cherished mother, and the pain of it still haunted her. "I'm sorry."

She nodded, her eyes suspiciously bright, before she briskly returned to her task. "She's not in pain anymore. So it was a blessing of sorts."

"True," he agreed, the urge to comfort her so strong he had to clench his fists to keep them from reaching for her. "But it doesn't make the grief any easier to bear."

"No."

He watched her in silence as she swallowed and then busied herself with her already-hung clothing.

"Maybe it's good that you're spending the holidays with us, instead of being alone in Oregon," he suggested quietly.

She blinked and sniffed before offering him a tremulous smile. "Leave it to you to frame this as a blessing."

He smiled back, his chest suspiciously warm and tight. "Are there any holiday traditions you'd like us to include? Anything to help you remember your mother?"

"Oh, we never did anything out of the ordinary," she said with a small shake of her head. "We decorated a tree, shared a family dinner and exchanged inexpensive gifts."

"Well, we can offer the family dinner, at least," he said, extending a palm. "And company to help you feel less alone."

CHAPTER SEVEN

WHEN LAURA and Kyros entered the dining room with Titus for their Christmas meal, it was to find a feast spread out on a large, polished table that looked as if it had hosted a thousand state meals. Toward one end, a traditional meze platter was piled high with olives, cheese, wedges of pita and stuffed grape leaves. Arranged next to the appetizers, a mouthwatering display of roasted lamb with potatoes, stuffed turkey, salads and ornate loaves of decorated bread made Laura realize she was famished.

Iona looked up from her wheelchair and waved them to their seats. "Come. Come," she urged with a smile. "I've had a chair set up for Titus, too." She gestured toward an assortment of spoons and miniscule tidbits of pita she'd arranged on his tray. "I assume you've started him on solids?"

Laura moved to the highchair and angled Titus's plump legs into its seat. He immediately set about banging on the tray while she adjusted his belt and tucked a bib around his neck. Within seconds, he'd swept the spoons and half the pita bits to the floor.

She bent to retrieve the spoons and winced. "Sorry about that."

"Do not be!" Iona answered with a smile as the spoons clattered to the floor yet again. "Titus only plays to play and I adore him for it."

Kyros bent to kiss the top of his grandmother's gray head as Laura claimed the chair closest to Titus. "He'll play to win soon enough. Don't you worry."

"Worry? That is exactly what concerns me!" Iona's scowl held a hint of humor as she reached for another spoon to place on Titus's tray. "I see this darling boy of yours likes to throw things almost as much as you did. It is only a matter of time before he starts to order people about."

"I hope so. Ordering people about is an important skill," Kyros said as he pushed Laura's chair in and then claimed the seat next to hers. "It lets people know who's in charge."

"Claims the man who is *always* in charge," Iona quipped.

"It gets me where I want to go, doesn't it?"

Iona cocked her head. "If you do not mind making a few enemies along the way, yes."

"Giagiá!" he said with feigned shock. "I don't have enemies. I have only business associates who refuse to care for me."

Iona shot Laura a telling glance. "It is a good thing he is so handsome, no? Otherwise, all the women would hate him, too."

"No one can afford to hate me," Kyros said as he leaned to load his plate with an assortment of appetizers. "I make them too much money."

Titus squealed in apparent agreement, banging both palms against his tray until Laura distracted him with a raisin.

"Money cannot replace relationships," Iona said. She smiled as Titus groped unsuccessfully for the raisin with his tiny fingers. "It is important to be considerate and kind, as well."

"I'm considerate and kind," Kyros protested. He angled a look toward Laura, a wicked gleam of teasing making his eyes dance with green fire. "Tell *Giagiá* how sweet and docile I am."

Laura winced, her guilt at deceiving the sweet old woman surging anew.

Iona's quiet huff of laughter saved her from answering. "Do not ask Lana to lie, my dear boy. It is obvious she is uncomfortable with deception."

Worried that Iona might see *too* much of the truth, Laura rushed to say, "Kyros is a wonderful man, Iona. I have no complaints at all."

She arched a silver brow. "So he leaves his competitive barracuda tendencies at the office?"

"Of course I do," Kyros said, leaning to loop an arm over Laura's shoulder. He hauled her close and tipped her face up with one commanding finger beneath her chin. "With my lovely wife and magnificent son, I am a tender, lovelorn sap." He grazed her mouth with his and then pulled back with a triumphant smile. "Isn't that right?"

Her mouth tingling and her brain somewhat dazed, Laura simply nodded.

Kyros straightened and then grinned back at his grandmother. "Besides, there is no need for competition with my beautiful wife. No one is in charge, we're both deliriously happy, and we *both* win."

Iona cocked her head and then slowly smiled, her gaze skipping from Laura's flushed face to her grandson and back. "This is exactly what I had hoped for you," she said. "To find a woman who loves you and who softens all those hard edges of yours."

Kyros's thumb traced the top of Laura's arm while he smiled back at his grandmother. "You always knew what was best for me, didn't you?"

"And it only took you thirty-six years to agree with me." Iona reached for a bottle and lifted it between them. "I would like to make a toast," she said.

"Are you sure it won't interfere with your medicines?" Kyros asked as worry creased his brow.

"I'll just have a little," Iona said with a wave of her free hand. "Not enough to cause any problems."

"Water it down," he warned as he slid their glasses toward Iona.

"But water will ruin the ouzo," Iona protested.

"Too bad."

Iona huffed out an aggrieved sigh, exchanging a look with Laura. "Can you not believe how bossy he is?"

Laura nodded as Iona diluted their drinks. "It changed color," Laura said in wonder as the clear liquid turned opaque.

"It reacts with the water," Kyros told her, handing Laura her glass. "But it will taste just the same."

"Almost," Iona grumbled.

"To my *Giagiá*," Kyros said with a warm smile as he lifted his glass. "For her willingness to drink watered-down ouzo just to keep her grandson's worries at bay."

Iona blinked, her eyes turning misty as she raised her glass, as well. "To Christmas, to family and to the woman who finally brought Kyros happiness. Thank you for creating such a beautiful son so that my own dear Titus's legacy can continue for yet another generation."

Despite the lump forming in her throat, Laura joined in the toast. "To Christmas," she repeated. After the clink of glasses and an exchange of misty smiles, Laura brought the ouzo to her lips. She fought a cough as the fiery, licorice-flavored alcohol burned its path down her throat.

Kyros, who'd been watching her over his own glass, grinned at her efforts. "It has a kick, doesn't it?"

At a loss for words, Laura blinked back a sting of tears and nodded.

"She will learn soon enough to drink her ouzo," Iona said. "Every proper Greek wife does."

"*Giagiá*," Kyros said as he lowered his glass and surveyed the groaning table. "You do realize, don't you, that there's

enough food here to feed all of Greece. Is someone else coming that I didn't know about?"

Iona dismissed his comment with a flutter of her thin fingers. "You know me," she replied. "Once I start preparing a
meal, I cannot stop."

Laura viewed the generous spread with awe. "You prepared all of this yourself?"

Iona eyed her grandson and then sighed. "No. Not anymore. We have a cook, Helen. Actually, she used to work
with me, and she stayed on as the estate cook when Kyros
bought the island. I'm afraid I cannot claim any of the credit
this time."

"This time?"

"Didn't Kyros tell you I used to be the head cook here?
That I once prepared banquets for dignitaries and princes
and kings?"

Laura's fork stalled above her plate as she turned to Kyros
for clarification. "Iona *worked* here?"

He answered with a short nod. "Until I made her retire."

"He bought the place out from under my employers so I
had no choice," Iona interrupted.

"You were nearly seventy years old," Kyros reminded her.

"Kyros!" Iona scolded. "It is impolite to discuss a woman's age."

"It's also impolite to be stubborn for no good reason,"
he answered without a hint of rancor. "No grandmother of
mine should have to work as a servant if she doesn't have to."

"There is no shame in doing a servant's job," she answered
archly before angling a look at Laura. "You watch out for this
boy, dear. He has enough pride for twenty men."

"Wanting my grandmother to relax and enjoy the final
years of her life is not pride. It's love and concern."

"Love and concern?" she echoed with an arched brow
before leaning toward Laura to clarify. "The wretched boy
forced me to choose between retirement and my home."

"Exactly." A fond smile creased his green eyes. "And look at what a marvelous choice you made."

"You are a bully," she said with a disgruntled tsking sound.

"Yes, I suppose I am." He shrugged. "But at least I know how to get what I want."

Iona served a plate of lamb and potatoes and then slid it toward Laura with a warm, yet exasperated glance. "You are a brave woman to marry Kyros," she said. "Perhaps you will succeed where I have failed and teach this man that he has limits."

"I have no limits," he countered with verbal swagger. "Those who think I do quickly learn otherwise."

His grandmother served a second plate of lamb and potatoes before sliding it to Kyros. "I seem to remember Achilles saying the same thing," she warned. "And look what happened to him."

Kyros laughed, holding up a hand in protest. "I surrender. You, oh wise one, are correct. I am flawed and afflicted with debilitating pride. So why don't we eat our Christmas feast before you scare my bride away?"

And with that, the feast began in earnest, until Laura felt she'd eaten enough for ten holidays. Thirty minutes later, after putting Titus down for bed and sipping another glass of ouzo, Laura felt warm and dangerously relaxed as they lingered over their desserts. Laura was enchanted by the obvious affection between Kyros and his grandmother. Exquisitely aware of Kyros's warm body next to hers, she found that the thought of sharing a room with Kyros didn't bother her nearly as much as it should.

"You must try one of *Giagiá's melomakarona* pastries," Kyros said, nudging the plate of walnut-encrusted cookies toward Laura. "They're delicious."

"I can't eat another thing," she protested with a hand against her stomach.

"Of course you can. There's always room for dessert," he

urged, lifting one of the honey-soaked cookies to her mouth. "C'mon. Just one bite."

Not wanting to be rude, she obliged him by accepting a small bite. Surprised by the unusual blend of spices, she closed her eyes for a moment to savor the spicy clove and cinnamon flavors. When she opened them, it was to find Kyros's attention riveted on her mouth.

"You're right," she said, licking her lips and swallowing. "Those are amazing."

"You missed a spot," he told her, gesturing toward her mouth with a distracted flick of his fingers. "There's still some...*melomakarona* on your..." He cleared his throat and blinked, his words trailing off.

Before her wayward thoughts convinced her that Kyros was staring at her with hunger in his eyes, she brushed the crumbs from her mouth and shifted her attention to his grandmother. "You must give me the recipe," she said. "And perhaps, in the morning, you and Helen can give me a baking lesson or two."

"I will teach you my bread recipe," Iona said, casting a glance toward Kyros. "If you can fix my grandson a good loaf of bread, he will be your slave forever."

"I am already her slave," he said with an intense stare at Laura's mouth. He leaned toward her and looped his long arm over the back of her chair. "Aren't I, *glykiá mou*?"

With Kyros so close, Laura was sorely tempted to wilt into the cove of his arm and chest. She wanted that broad expanse of muscle, bone and sinew all along her side, his scent in her nostrils and his taste in her mouth. Horrified by the train of her thoughts, she stiffened beneath the glancing touch of his fingers against her neck and forced her attention back to the topic at hand. "I'm afraid my baking skills leave much to be desired," she told Iona. "But I will certainly do my best."

"Trust me," Kyros whispered. "You more than make up for it with your other...talents."

The suggestive undercurrent of his delivery sent a torrent of heat along the surface of her skin. "Kyros," she scolded under her breath as she stole a look at Iona's pleased expression. "You're embarrassing me."

"I can't help it," he confessed with an unrepentant smile. "You bring out the rogue in me." He moved his warm palm to her neck and brushed a thumb along the tense muscles of her nape. "Forgive me?" he asked as he looked down at her.

His remarkable green eyes, their thick, curling lashes and the glinting flecks of silver deep within the clear jade trapped her, rendering her incapable of retreat. For a moment, she felt as if she were falling into a mysterious green pond with untold depths. The dizzying sensation coiled within her belly and she stopped breathing, suspended in his clear gaze.

"She forgives you," Iona said, breaking the spell with a soft laugh. "So now why don't you tell me how the two of you met?"

"We met at a business cocktail party," Kyros answered before slowly averting his gaze. His fingers returned to her nape and squeezed while his voice lowered to an intimate hum. "I saw her across the room, and immediately knew she was the only one for me."

"I always knew you were a romantic," his grandmother said. "You have too much of your grandfather in you not to be."

"Well, it sure surprised me," Kyros answered, and his velvet voice sent a shiver of awareness down Laura's spine. "One minute in her presence, and I was sunk. All my hopes for a happy future lay within her beautiful hands."

Glancing back at him, Laura read the look in his eyes. The raw glimmer of heat sent surges of anxiety and excitement winnowing along the surface of her skin. When had any man, let alone one with Kyros's masculine appeal, ever looked at her with such appetite and interest? *It's not real,*

she reminded herself. *Just like you, he's pretending for his grandmother's sake.*

His warm gaze tracked her face, her parted lips, and her tingling breasts, bringing a flush of prickling awareness to her veins. It was the kind of stare a husband gave a wife, or a man gave to his lover, and it unsettled her. Because it didn't look like he was faking. It looked real. It *felt* real.

"And what about you?" Iona asked, turning to Laura with a web of happy lines gathering at the corners of her eyes. "Did you fall in love with Kyros at first sight as well?"

Laura licked her lips, her awareness of Kyros's warm hand against her flesh making it difficult to concentrate. "I think half the world has fallen in love at first sight with your grandson," she admitted.

Iona's featured softened even further while her approving smile encompassed them both. "What a lovely thing to say. Kyros is lucky to have you loving him, Lana. While *I* am lucky you both have chosen to share your holidays with an old, ailing woman."

Kyros's smooth voice joined in as he said, "We wouldn't have missed your holiday celebrations for the world."

"No?" his grandmother asked. "The parties I host now do not compare to all those glamorous business affairs you attend."

"Fortunately, Lana prefers warmth to glamour," he said. "Isn't that right, *agápi mou?*"

Iona laughed before Laura could answer, her pleasure at the comment evident in her soft smile. "Tell me the truth, dear," she said, directing her question to Laura, "what did this boy do to get you to abandon Athens for the holidays?"

"He didn't have to do anything," Laura assured her while memories of their bargaining and subsequent kiss fired her cheeks. "I love small family celebrations, and couldn't wait to meet the grandmother I've heard so much about."

"Did you now?"

"Absolutely," Laura insisted. "I can't imagine a better holiday than one spent in your lovely home."

Iona laughed again, shifting her attention to Kyros. "No wonder you eloped. You would never have the patience to wait for the more traditional arrangements."

"You're right," he answered. "The very night she agreed to my proposal, I whisked her to Vegas and the deed was done."

"I suppose I can forgive you for not inviting me, then," Iona said with a long-suffering sigh. "Though I do wish I could have been there regardless."

"I wish you could have been there, too," Laura said, hauling her attention from Kyros back to Iona.

"Tell me you had a wonderful honeymoon, and I shall be mollified."

"We had a perfect honeymoon," Kyros said before Laura could answer. He lifted Laura's hand to his mouth and kissed her knuckles while staring deep into her eyes. She read the raw desire simmering within the pale green and shivered. "Didn't we?" he murmured in a husky voice.

Laura swallowed and blinked, her pulse fluttering wildly beneath her skin. "Kyros…"

"As long as the honeymoon has lasted beyond Vegas and you do not spend all your time on business," Iona said to Kyros, "I will not attempt to give you marriage advice."

"*Giagiá,*" Kyros began.

"Because I know you, and nothing will drive a marriage into the ground faster than a husband who is too busy to pay attention to his wife."

"Kyros is not too busy," Laura lied, her entire body hot. "He is quite attentive and loving."

"And he makes you happy?"

"Very much so," Laura murmured.

"Good. Because you must not leave him after I am gone. You must remember that he loves you, even when he forgets to behave as if he does."

"Giagiá!" Kyros scolded.

"What?" Iona answered as she cast an unapologetic glance at him. "You get to be my age, you realize that love and family are the most important gifts you can share. You realize that you must cultivate your happiness, and never take it for granted."

"I won't."

"You will. You find mountains just so you can climb them, no matter who you leave behind, and I want Lana to be prepared."

He flushed and the muscles in his jaw flexed. "Lana knows I love her. She knows I won't leave her behind."

"I am happy to hear it."

Laura thought of Kyros's tightly coiled energy, and how his underlying aggression seemed to simmer beneath the surface even when he appeared relaxed. Perhaps that's why he fascinated her the way he did. He did need someone to temper all that energy, to soften the edges of his relentless drive. But it certainly couldn't be her. She was merely a substitute for the wife he needed, an imposter.

Iona turned to face Laura. "Lana?"

"Yes?"

"You must remember this promise Kyros makes tonight. Remind him of it when he tries to push you away."

"Giagiá—"

"Because he will push you away. It is what he does. But I want you to have faith in his love for you. No matter what, trust that he loves you."

"Okay," Laura whispered.

Kyros's harsh features softened, and a note of exasperated affection colored his tone. "Enough, *Giagiá.* I thought you said you wouldn't offer marriage advice."

"I have said my piece," Iona said. "My hope is that you both have listened."

To Laura's relief, the conversation turned to other topics.

Kyros kept her ouzo glass filled as they talked, and as the Christmas night stretched toward midnight, Laura drifted in and out of the conversation with an ease she wouldn't have anticipated.

It's because you're drunk, she realized with a small frisson of surprise. She'd never been drunk before, but rather than being embarrassed, she felt oddly warm and relaxed.

Puzzled, she stared at her nearly full glass, trying to remember how many times it had been refilled. Straightening to scold Kyros for getting her drunk, she was startled to discover the room had tilted. She listed left, the table before her rising up to meet her with startling speed. Kyros caught her before she collided with the dark wood, steadying her in one quicksilver move. Laura blinked, his closeness reminding her of how lovely it had been to feel his lips against hers.

"Kyros," she scolded, her lips feeling loose and her unwieldy tongue not cooperating at all. "You gave me too much ouzo."

"Three drinks over three hours." His beautiful mouth hitched with humor. "I didn't think you were *that* much of a lightweight."

She lolled her head left, trying to focus on Iona's amused eyes. "Your grandson got me drunk," she accused.

"I imagine he has designs on your virtue," observed Iona with a warm chuckle.

The thought sent Laura lurching to her feet. The room didn't quite cooperate with the change in her position, spinning and tilting dangerously as she tried to retain her balance. She felt herself tipping sideways, tumbling helplessly toward the floor.

Kyros vaulted up to catch her, banding his arm about her waist and steadying her against the bulwark of his muscled body.

"Oh—" Laura splayed her hand against his hard chest, pressing upright and then peering blurrily up at him. "I'm

sorry. I didn't expect to be so dizzy." Her gaze shifted to his wide, wide chest and her small hand upon it. She became aware of the contrast between their sizes, and the thought of his big body plundering hers had every inch of skin humming with longing.

"She really is a tiny hummingbird of a girl, is she not?" Iona observed.

"Yes," Kyros agreed with a soft chuckle. "But she's my hummingbird." He smiled down at Laura, his eyes perilously, disturbingly heated despite their teasing glimmer of green. "Aren't you, *glykiá mou?*"

Faint with the desire to agree with him, but not *quite* drunk enough to verbalize her foolishness, she narrowed her eyes and tried to press free of his arms.

"Careful." He retained his hold on her and gently spun her toward the exit before angling his face back toward his grandmother. "I think we'll head up before she falls asleep on her feet. Do you have someone to help you to bed, or shall I come back?"

"Sandrine's expecting me. I told her I'd be in around midnight."

"Good night, then. We'll see you in the morning."

Laura and Kyros made it about halfway to their suite, Laura's steps a disjointed blend of stumble and stall, until he bent to lift her in his strong arms.

"What are you doing?" she gasped as she looped a steadying arm around his neck.

"Carrying my wife to bed." He stared at her, his expression dangerously serious. "And maybe I'll be the unprincipled ogre you believe me to be and ravish you while you're helpless to resist."

"I'm not help…" Laura licked her lips, fully intending to scold the beautiful man who somehow had managed to get far, far too close. But somehow, her words got muddled and

she forgot what she'd meant to say. "You're not really going to ravish me, are you?"

"Would you like me to?" he asked, his green eyes glinting with a scalding heat.

She considered the question, tilting her head as she stared longingly at his mouth. After a few seconds of torturous indecision, she sighed disconsolately. "No," she said faintly.

"Are you sure?" His question drifted perilously close to her mouth, his hot breath kissing her sensitive lips and igniting a knot of fire deep within her belly. "Because afterward, when you felt guilty, you could pretend you don't remember."

She considered his suggestion, her fuzzy logic competing rather ineffectually against her desire to test his theory. "I still don't think it's a good idea."

"Don't you?" The wicked gleam in his eyes tempted her into reconsidering.

She shook her head and then immediately regretted it, her resolve wavering as readily as the walls. "No. I'd never forgive myself." Trying to sound firm, she excavated additional reasons from the recesses of her cloudy thoughts. "Or you. I'd have to leave. And I'd never see Titus again." She frowned, realizing they'd arrived at their opulent gold suite. "That would make me very, very sad."

"Yes. I do believe you're right," he said, sounding disappointed but resolute as he laid her upon the big, white bed. She looked up at his dark face as he leaned over her, her hands lax beside her head and her left thigh pressed against his hip.

"I still have my shoes on," she told him, and the words seemed to leave her mouth like dandelion seeds on a summer breeze. "And my clothes."

"Yes. I noticed." Kyros's face seemed very, very close, and his eyes gleamed with an intensity that stole her breath. "Shall I take them off for you?"

She considered his question, fuzzily aware of how hot

she felt, of how intoxicated she was, and of how impaired her judgment must be. "I...I don't think that's a good idea," she said, faltering.

"I won't take advantage," he told her. "I just want to make you comfortable."

"I'm already..." Her voice trailed off as his head lowered over hers and she realized she didn't care about what she may or may not regret. She wanted him to kiss her. Now. She wanted him to undress her, to trail his hot hands over her burning flesh and teach her all the things about her body she'd yet to learn. She held her breath and waited, her eyes searching his while tingling anticipation built within her veins.

She felt his fingers pluck at the buttons of her jacket, shifting her from side to side as he gently drew the blazer down her arms. When she was stripped to her silk blouse, his hands moved to her skirt and shoes. The velvet slide of his fingers along her abdomen, thighs and calves sent an erotic shiver over her skin, and her foot twitched involuntarily as he withdrew first one navy pump, and then the other. When she lay beneath him, he bent to press a glancing kiss against her brow. She arched toward him, reaching blindly for his mouth. But he withdrew, his features taut and his eyes dark with need.

"You need to rest," he told her. "I know you didn't sleep at all last night."

"I'm not tired," she whispered.

"Perhaps not. But you *are* drunk."

"Just a little bit."

"It's enough."

Breathing unsteadily, she lifted her wrist to her eyes. "You're right. Perhaps you should go."

"Yes."

"Kyros?"

"Yes?"

"Thank you for…for not ravishing me."

His gaze skimmed her disheveled body from head to toe before tugging the blanket up over her. "You're welcome."

"And I was wrong about you. You're not an ogre."

He nodded and then straightened, his hands balled into fists at his sides. "No, I'm not," he muttered in a low voice. "I'm a damn saint."

CHAPTER EIGHT

LATER THE following morning, after a pleasant baking lesson with Iona and Helen, Laura returned to her suite to put Titus down for his nap. She was surprised to find Kyros there, dressed in dark slacks and a white shirt with its collar undone. He'd rolled up his cuffs, revealing muscled forearms the color of teak, and he sat in one of the white-and-gold striped chairs with his laptop balanced on one bent leg.

"Titus needs a nap," she told him, her gaze flickering to his laptop and then back. "You don't mind if I come in to put him down, do you?"

"Of course not." He looked pleased to see them despite the interruption. Waving them farther into the room, he closed his laptop with a click and then rose from his chair. "I just finished."

Laura tensed at his approach, and her pulse kicked up a notch as he drew near. Despite her drunkenness last night, she remembered her behavior with disconcerting clarity. Particularly the way she'd lost her inhibitions and practically begged Kyros to kiss her.

She remembered, too, how easily he resisted her. He'd left her in her solitary bed without any apparent regret, and seeing him now sent a wave of humiliation flooding through her limbs.

Thankfully, he didn't appear to be in the mood to tease

her about it. Instead, he merely stopped, smiled down at his son and raised a large, square hand to stroke Titus's rounded cheek.

"Hey there, sailor, are you getting cranky?" He bent close to kiss the top of Titus's dark head, and Laura's gaze darted to Kyros's thick, black curls.

A flash of longing to touch his hair made her hand tighten against Titus's warmed bottle as Kyros withdrew enough for her to breathe. "Not at all," Laura managed to say. "He's been a doll all morning. He helped us make bread."

Kyros's emerald gaze lifted to hers. "Bread?" he teased. "Are you trying to make me your slave, Laura?"

She blushed. "Of course not. It was Iona who chose the recipe for my lesson."

"Well, I can't wait to taste it." He grinned down at his son. "How about you, Titus?"

Titus rubbed his ear with a knotted fist, and then turned to burrow into Laura's shoulder with a whimper.

Laura glanced down at the warm bundle of tired baby and added, "I think the only thing he can't wait for is a nap."

"You need some shut-eye, hmm?" he said to Titus.

She felt Kyros's attention shift to her, and kept her gaze fastened on Titus. Looking at Kyros, with his face so close to hers, would be unwise.

"I don't remember the last time I spent an afternoon in bed," he observed in a silky voice. His finger crooked beneath her chin and tipped her face up. "How about you?"

"N-no." Her chest tightened against her breath and for a moment, she was awash in dizzying impressions: dark skin, emerald eyes, a shadow of close-shaven beard and a scent so appealing and alluring, she nearly swayed. Disconcerted by her reaction, she took a stumbling step back. "I don't have time for naps."

"Did I say anything about a nap?" he teased.

Knowing he was trying to shock her, she fought the wave

of heat that climbed her cheeks. "Kyros," she scolded. "You are being entirely inappropriate."

"I know," he agreed without a hint of contrition. "You should try it some time."

She scowled and then ducked around him, heading toward Titus's room. "Titus is tired. I need to feed him his bottle and put him down."

He watched her hasty retreat, stopping to lounge against the door frame as she settled into the rocker. "You're fun to tease," he said. His gaze flashed with a hint of challenge, daring her to deny him his bit of entertainment.

"Well, I wish you wouldn't," she said crisply. Lana might have been good at the games men like Kyros played, but she wasn't. She didn't know the first thing about flirting, and pretending otherwise made her feel awkward and tongue-tied. "It makes me uncomfortable."

Kyros simply stared at her with that unnerving smile of his, as if making her uncomfortable were his favorite task of the day. Disconcerted, she dipped her head and fussed with Titus, adjusting his position in her lap and angling the bottle into his mouth. Titus grabbed it with both hands and his sounds of contented, eager sucking soon filled the room.

"You're good with him," Kyros said after a few moments. His voice sounded like the swish of raw silk against flesh within the room's quietness. "Better than I thought you'd be."

"He's a very easy baby," she replied without lifting her eyes. But even without looking at Kyros, she felt his presence. And she felt her own burning awareness of him, as well. It perturbed her, this fascination he held for her. His scent—the combination of wood smoke, sea, starched cotton and a hint of morning coffee—affected her powerfully, and it worried her. He was Lana's widower. He was completely, utterly, no questions asked, off-limits.

"I've decided I want you to stay on as Titus's nanny once your eight days have elapsed," he said.

Startled, she looked up at him. His expression offered no clue as to what he was thinking, or if he'd meant the offer in jest. "Why?"

He answered with a slow shrug. "Are you interested?"

Recklessness and caution immediately took up arms, gathering reinforcements from every corner of her body. "I…"

"You don't have to decide now," he said before her common sense could assert itself. "Just think about it."

She suspected her consternation must have shown on her face, because his eyes glimmered with humor as he strode closer to brace his hands around the ornate finials on each side of the rocker's curved back. "Relax, Laura," he told her in a teasing whisper as he bent low over her face, "I didn't ask you to be my mistress."

She gasped, rearing away from the warmth of his breath, and then fixed him with a reproachful glance. "Well, if you're trying to convince me," she whispered back, "this is hardly the way to go about it."

He looked deep into her eyes, his own so close, she could see each individual spiked lash. "Are you sure?"

Laura stared at him in dismay, her heart thumping noisily. "Yes, I'm sure," she whispered primly, deciding her best defense was to respond with a rational reminder of the boundaries between them. "You know full well that I would love to spend more time with Titus. But to imply that I would consider being your mistress is both inappropriate and wrong."

"Such ruffled feathers," he soothed. "I didn't mean to offend you."

"Well, you did," she said firmly as she hiked her chin. "Though Lana and I were estranged, she was my sister. To suggest that I would somehow become…*involved* with her husband dishonors both her memory and me and—"

"I apologize," he interrupted, looking not at all penitent. "I won't do it again. I promise."

"See that you don't," she scolded with a small frown be-

fore shifting her attention back to Titus, who'd already fallen asleep. She removed the bottle from his slack mouth and reached to set it on the small table at her right elbow. Then she shifted her weight as she prepared to rise, scooting forward on the rocking chair's bowed feet and glancing meaningfully at the braced arms prohibiting her exit. "Do you mind? I need to put Titus down."

Rather than accommodate her request, Kyros pressed the chair backward, tipping the rocker onto its heels. The unexpected motion brought Laura's toes off the floor and tilted the carved oak of the chair's back high against her nape. With her knot of hair smashed against the wood, her arms wrapped around a sleeping Titus, and her feet adrift, she felt positively unmoored. "What are you doing?" she gasped with a startled whisper.

"Taking advantage of an opportunity," he murmured as he lifted the fingers of one hand to smooth her knotted forehead. "What else?"

"Release me," she said as she flattened herself against the wooden slats of the ornate rocker's back.

"Why should I?" he asked, a thread of amusement humming in his voice.

Her heartbeat kicked into high gear, making her sweater constrict against her throat. As she tried to swallow her reaction back, he stared at her until his smile slowly faded.

His hand drifted to her cheek while his voice turned to velvet. "You take things too seriously, Laura Talbot," he said without taking his eyes from hers. "Keeping your thoughts and feelings so buttoned up all the time isn't healthy. And it won't make you happy."

"I *am* happy!" she protested, yanking her face free of his touch.

"Are you." He didn't ask it as a question, as if by framing the words as a statement would somehow grant her permission to disagree.

"Yes."

His eyes held hers, his expression one of quiet admonishment. "I thought you said you didn't lie."

"You've only known me for four days!" she protested.

"It's long enough." It felt almost as if he moved in slow motion, his finger and thumb lightly caressing a stray wisp of hair that had escaped its moorings. "I know you want things. Things you won't admit aloud."

"I don't want anything."

"But unlike your sister," he said as he slowly wrapped the fine strand around his index finger, "you're very, very good at hiding what those things are."

She knew she should refute him, that she should say something to call a halt to this madness. But those intense green eyes and his velvet voice hypnotized her into silence.

"A man likes a woman he can read," he murmured while he tucked the fine strand behind her ear, his fingertip and the grazing touch of his knuckle creating a burning trail of sensation along its delicate whorl. "A woman who can reveal her secrets when the occasion warrants. Like last night, after you'd drunk a bit of ouzo."

No, she thought. *That wasn't me.* But she sat immobile, mesmerized, as he tracked the curling floss of hair beneath her earlobe and along the fragile ridge of her jaw. She tried not to think about the kiss they'd shared, about all the places on her body she wanted that finger to explore. Staring up at him with her heart in her throat, she said not a single word while her errant pulse ricocheted to every part of her wayward body.

"I've never seen anyone try so hard to keep her true self hidden," he observed in that low voice of his. His finger smoothed first one eyebrow and then the other, studying her face like a curious observer trying to puzzle out the reasons behind her expression. "Why is that, do you suppose?"

She said nothing, letting him do what he would with those

clever fingers of his. He traced a feather-light caress from her brow to the heated crest of her cheek, and shivers raced across her belly.

"What are you afraid I'll find?" he asked as he drew languorous submission to her puckered brow.

This. "Kyros," she beseeched, "please let me down."

His teeth flashed white while his hot gaze flicked to her mouth and back. "What if I don't want to?"

"Then I'll scream," she said faintly.

"And wake Titus?" He grazed the slope of her upturned throat with a single finger, trailing fire along the sensitive flesh. "I don't think so."

She couldn't believe he was touching her, tormenting her, and offering her no avenue of escape. "You're doing it again," she told him in a breathless attempt at indignation.

"It?"

"Using Titus to get what you want."

"Ah. But it's what you want, too, isn't it?" he assured her without a hint of remorse.

She frowned, steeling herself against the seductive appeal of his touch. "No. I don't want this with you. I don't want anything from you besides access to Titus."

"You don't?" His wicked green eyes dared her to repeat the lie.

Hitching her chin and forcing a fierceness to her whisper, she reiterated all the rational reasons she'd been rehearsing. "No. I don't. You're Lana's widower. My sister's *husband.* Any sort of affair between us would ruin everything."

"How?"

"I could never stay as Titus's nanny if we…if you…it would be…"

"It would be…?" he prodded. He leaned further forward, until Laura arched as far from him as the chair would allow. "What would it be, *glykiá mou?*"

"Wrong," she told him, fighting to draw air into her lungs.

It was too hot. Too close. Her head felt too heavy to lift from the back of the chair, the effects of gravity and Kyros's nearness weighing her inhibitions and making her body feel perilously languid and relaxed. "It would be wrong," she protested feebly.

"It's only wrong if you don't desire me," he said. His dark face hovered over hers, close enough that she could see the faint flecks of silver in his emerald eyes, while his mouth, that beautiful, tantalizing, *tempting* mouth waited mere inches from hers. "Tell me you don't desire me, and I'll release you," he said, and she felt the heat of his exhalation against her cheek.

"Of course I…I don't desire you," she said, faltering.

"No?" He withdrew enough for her to see the subtle hint of amusement curving his lips.

"No…I…" Her voice drifted into silence as his head slowly lowered over hers, and she closed her eyes as a fierce, tingling knot of arousal rose to beat within her chest. She felt his breath caress her trembling lips, a sweet, drugging infusion of mint and coffee and *him,* and waited while anticipation coiled tightly in her veins. Slowly, slowly, she felt his mouth brush the delicate skin beneath her right eye and then her left. The gentle contact, as fleeting as it was forbidden, sent a shiver along her nerve endings and she felt herself turn toward him. He deftly avoided her, skirting her mouth to drift lower, then lower still, until the lingering slide of tongue and lip met the soft, thin skin beneath her jaw. Her pulse beat wildly, while her entire body went taut. She wanted to reach for him, to drag his mouth to hers and forget about all the reasons she shouldn't.

Just when she thought she could bear it no longer, he lifted his dark head and stared at her with eyes gone opaque with need.

"Convince me you don't desire me," he rasped softly, "tell me so I believe it."

It scared her, how much she wanted to admit the truth. But it would ruin everything, she thought dizzily. An affair between them would be wrong. Horrible, wonderful, painful, exquisite and wrong. Wrong.

"Please don't do this," she begged.

He continued to stare down at her, unsmiling, as the silence beat between them.

"I...I need to put Titus down," she told him in a shaky voice. "Before he wakes up."

His expression remained inscrutable, but when he spoke, his voice sounded ragged. "Of course you do."

He bent his arms, slowly guiding the rocking chair back down and then stepping back. Once her toes touched the floor, Laura clambered to her feet, turning away from the inviting closeness of his hard, warm body. "I don't think we should be alone anymore," she said as she moved toward the rails of Titus's crib.

You're right. Kyros watched Laura ease Titus into his crib and then escape the room, her disconcerted expression and flushed face a testament to how much he'd unnerved her. It left him with an uncomfortable blend of irritation and regret. He knew he'd pushed further than he should have, but his desire to delve beneath her protective shell had overwhelmed his common sense.

His hunger for her seemed to blind him to rational thought and render him incapable of controlling himself. Watching her with his son, so attentive and gentle, had sparked a desire he didn't want to acknowledge. A desire he had no business feeling. Not for his wife's twin sister. Not for anyone. It was an agony he'd never before encountered, and he was out of his depth. He'd never once felt compelled to pursue a woman he knew better than to want.

But if he'd learned anything in the past few days, it was that he wanted Laura. It didn't seem to matter that he didn't trust her. It didn't seem to matter that she was Lana's sis-

ter. Even knowing she hid her true self beneath the surface
sweetness she'd donned, even knowing she couldn't possibly
be the woman she pretended to be, his body couldn't seem
to heed the warnings of his brain. He wanted her. Beneath
him. Around him. Gasping out his name as he lost himself
deep inside her.

The realization did not sit well in his gut.

CHAPTER NINE

Two days later, after which Laura had avoided being alone with him at all, Kyros felt ready to chew the walls down to dust. He couldn't remember the last time he'd functioned under such a constant state of frustrated arousal. So when *Giagiá* informed him of her New Year's Eve plans, he leapt at the opportunity to legitimately spend time with Laura. Alone. Touching her. Demystifying the feminine puzzle he'd yet to figure out.

"Would you mind keeping an eye on Titus while I teach Lana how to dance the *kalamatian?*" he asked *Giagiá*.

"Of course not. I will send her to the ballroom while you get the music ready."

Five minutes later, Laura arrived at the empty ballroom wearing yet another of her drab brown suits. It wasn't particularly unattractive; it was just more proof of how she hid herself from the world, a fabric barricade she'd erected to keep him and his questions at bay.

Kyros wanted to tell her it didn't work, that he saw *her* despite her efforts to hide. But the claim would have been a lie. Yes, his body would recognize hers in the dark, but he knew *her* no more than he had six days ago. He hated it. She was still as much of a mystery, wrapped in a shell of sweet, sheltered innocence he couldn't delve beneath no matter how he tried.

What was it about her that intrigued him so much? Why couldn't he discern her motives when every other woman in the world was so easy to read?

With nothing more than a shy smile and a shrug of her narrow shoulder, she could send wild currents of arousal through his body. Without even appearing to try, she captivated him more than any other woman. And yet, even while she dismantled his defenses with nothing more than a glance, she remained frustratingly out of reach. It didn't make sense, but he wasn't foolish enough to underestimate his response to her. Whether his reaction was rational or not was immaterial. He wanted her.

And he wanted to know why. He wanted to dissect her appeal to him, analyze it, strip it of its power and then discard it before she drove him mad.

Kyros watched Laura as she approached, her posture straight and prim and her smile a bit nervous. Her shirt, a silky fabric the color of creamed coffee, was a study in modesty beneath her sturdy, serviceable blazer. And yet, just above its top button, he caught a glimpse of her pale throat. The tiny dip at its base, that shallow indentation of tender skin that trembled with her pulse, riveted him.

He wanted to bury his face against that flash of skin and kiss her. Taste her. Devour her. Thoughts of all the things he wanted to do with the small body she insisted on hiding quickened his breath.

"You sent for me?" she asked, and he forced his thoughts and his attention to her bright, inquisitive face. Such a deceptively innocent face…why couldn't he see through to the woman beneath?

"*Giagiá* told me about her plans for New Year's Eve, and I thought you might wish to prepare."

Her features clouded with a hint of confusion. "Prepare how?"

"She's invited all of her friends and all the people who

knew me when I was growing up." He paused, staring down at her upturned face. "They believe they're coming to our wedding reception."

Her soft pink mouth dropped open. "*Our* wedding reception?"

He nodded. "It's *Giagiá*'s method of getting even for Lana's and my elopement." His mouth twisted into an apologetic smile. "She still hasn't forgiven me for leaving her out of the ceremony."

Her gaze skipped nervously from his face to his body and then back again. "Oh."

"So I thought I'd teach you a few of the traditional Greek dances we'll be expected to dance."

Her face blanched. "Everyone's going to watch us dance? Alone?"

"No," he assured her, though the thought of holding her close while their bodies brushed intimately together had him wishing there were a traditional couple's dance for just the two of them. "We mainly dance in a circle with everyone else. But I thought you'd like to know the steps ahead of time."

She caught her lower lip between her teeth while a pained look stole over her features. "I can't dance."

"Of course you can. The steps aren't complicated at all," he said, offering her an encouraging smile while confusion percolated in his brain. Why would she pretend she couldn't dance? What could *that* possibly gain her? "Once you have the basic pattern down, it's just the music that will change."

"No," she said, shaking her head as she backed toward the door. "I can't."

Her nervousness wrought a surge of protective pleasure within him. And maybe that was what she wanted. But suddenly, he didn't care. The idea of teaching her, of having her outwardly grateful for his tutelage even if it was a lie, was enough. "You can. I'll help you."

"No." She shook her head, her eyes filled with stark

worry. "You don't understand. I tried to dance once, and I was awful."

He arched a brow in surprise, marveling at her persistence. "You? Awful? I don't believe it."

"It's true. Miss Folliot did her best to teach me, but I never could get the hang of it."

"How old were you?"

"Six."

He scolded her with a disbelieving look. "Six."

Her mouth pursed into a defensive moue. "Yes, and all the other pupils managed just fine. Lana practically floated through the steps and her pliés were perfect. She'd laugh at my incompetence while I…" Her words trailed off, her train of thought visibly sent off course as he stepped closer. She cleared her throat. "What?"

"Lana laughed at you?"

"With good reason," she said. "I was awful. I was kicked out after only five lessons."

Suddenly, he could see the two of them as children, Lana's selfishness compelling her to denigrate and punish her sister for daring to compete with her. He suspected that even as children, Lana had been more abrasive than her softer twin. Laura's sweetness would have drawn adult praise like flowers drew bees, while Lana would have seemed spoiled and demanding by comparison. She'd have reacted with waspish spite and done everything in her power to strip Laura of any advantage she might claim. He reached for Laura's chin and tipped it up until he could stare deeply into her blue eyes. "Lana should have been whipped for—"

"She didn't mean any—"

"You have an innate grace, and anyone with eyes can see it."

Her gaze skirted his despite her tipped face, and he moved his hand to cup her fragile jaw. The electric sensation of her

smooth flesh against his palm caused his chest to tighten and his breath to catch. *How* could she affect him like this?

Laura inhaled sharply and stepped away from him. He stared down at her bowed head, aching to reach for her again, to burrow his fingers within that prim upsweep of sleek hair and tip her face back toward his. To convince her to let him inside. To trust him.

"If you tell me the name of the dances," she said unsteadily, "I'm sure I can look up the steps online and try to learn them on my own. There's no need to waste your time teaching me."

"I want to teach you." The husky timbre of his own voice surprised Kyros.

"But I won't…" She took a deep breath, appearing to gather her composure as he stared down at the top of her bent head. "I don't learn dance steps easily. I have no rhythm and I'll trample your feet. It will take forever to train me. You'll get frustrated and angry and I…"

"Why don't you let me be the judge of what frustrates me?" he admonished in a low voice.

She nodded miserably, staring at the floor between their feet.

"I'm supposed to be your husband, remember?" he said gruffly. "A besotted newlywed who will use any excuse to maximize his time with you."

She nodded quietly without looking at him, her hands knotted at her waist.

"Come here."

Her throat moved in a visible swallow and the color in her cheeks deepened before she gingerly moved back toward him. Against the backdrop of the elegant black-and-white ballroom, she looked like a small brown bird who'd stumbled into a lion's gilded lair. Above them, chandeliers glittered in the bright afternoon sun, dappling the checked marble floor with coins of rainbow light. The far wall of mirrors and win-

dows, curved like the Colosseum and twenty feet in height, offered alternating views of the winter seascape outside and Laura's narrow, brown back.

He wondered what she would look like wearing one of the low-cut numbers that seemed so popular, her cleavage visible and the rounded swells of her breasts edged by a silky ribbon of cobalt. He wanted to dress her in finery, to drape her neck and ears with sapphires and gold. He wanted to release her sleek, dark hair, to decorate her in the beauty of her own lush colors and curves.

"Shouldn't we have music?" she asked, forcing his thoughts back to their lesson.

"Not yet." He reached for her hand and lifted it until their arms were extended between them. "We'll work through the dance slowly a few times before we add the music."

"Okay," she said in a near-whisper.

With low, murmured words, he guided her through the steps of the *kalamatian*. Just as he'd anticipated, she followed his lead with effortless grace. It took her a few attempts to manage the seven-eighths time, but within ten minutes, she had mastered the popular dance.

"You haven't tried dancing since you were six years old, have you?" he asked.

She dropped her hands and shook her head wordlessly.

"Yet you've already learned the steps, in less time than it took me."

Her eyes glittered with a sheen of tears and he realized with a flash of insight that she hadn't lied about her experience with dancing. Had she spent her entire life fashioning an existence that would keep her safe from Lana's ridicule?

Was that why she hid herself from him the way she did?

Or was he so blinded by his own reaction to her that he couldn't reason objectively anymore?

Shaking off the thought, he said, "Let's try it with music, now." He strode to the sound system and cued up the playlist

of traditional Greek dance music, his mind and body humming with the prospect of touching her again. He wanted to crush her against him, make her body come alive beneath his hands, his mouth, and every straining inch of his aroused body. He wanted to show her that he understood her, that he knew everything about her despite her efforts to hide the truth from him.

But he kept himself in check, offering support and encouragement as they worked up to the quick pace of the music.

"Now, once people have had a bit to drink," he told her, "we'll stop holding hands and the circle will get tighter."

"How?" she asked in a breathy voice, her black lashes fluttering down over her blue eyes.

"Like this," he said. Kyros moved closer to and dropped his hand to the tidy notch of her waist. "Put your arm beneath mine and around my ribs." Though he'd danced with women a thousand times, having Laura tucked up against him while they moved together felt different. It felt…new. Her fingers against his ribs were insubstantial as sunlight, barely skimming his broad back, and he couldn't remember the last time he'd been so attuned to a woman's touch. "That's right," he murmured. "You've almost got it."

"My balance is off when we're this close," she protested.

"It's because you're trying too hard to maintain distance between us. If you let our hips and thighs touch, we won't keep colliding. Our movements will work together instead of fighting each other."

"I'm sorry." She pushed out of his arm and stopped a good meter from where he stood. "I can do it when we're just holding hands. That's good enough. Once everyone's drunk, nobody will notice if I bow out."

"*Giagiá* will."

She frowned, her eyes avoiding his. "Then I'll just say I'm tired."

"You'll lie?" he asked with an arched brow.

"It's not a lie," she insisted while color rose to her cheeks. "It's true. I haven't been sleeping well at all."

Neither had he. And listening to her toss and turn while he tried to get comfortable on a too-short couch had nearly done him in. "Then fake it. You're already pretending to be my wife. You may as well pretend to be well-rested while you're at it."

She bit her lip and scowled.

"You can do it if you just relax a bit," he coaxed. "Besides, no one will believe you're a suitable wife if you return to your seat just when the dancing gets good."

She closed her eyes and exhaled noisily, her scowl deepening. "Fine."

"Excellent." He moved back into position, arranging her arm across his back and curving his right hand over her rib cage, just beneath her breast. "Now with the next measure, we'll move right. That's it," he said. "Now left..."

To be honest, they moved awkwardly at first. She kept fighting his closeness, her focus on maintaining a sliver of space between their sides instead of on the steps, but he eventually convinced her to follow his lead. By the time they'd looped through the song an additional four times, she was gliding along with him in relaxed, if somewhat reluctant, conformity.

"See?" he gloated. "This isn't so bad, is it?"

She glared at him, though there was a glimmer of amusement beneath the faux display of temper. "Has anyone ever told you you're a bully?"

"All the time," he agreed easily.

"Don't you ever feel guilty for imposing your will on others?" she asked as they made a seamless transition from one direction to the other.

"Never."

"And you never doubt yourself."

"I know what I want and I go after it. Doubt only leads to indecision and weakness."

"But what if you're wrong?"

"I'd rather be wrong than be paralyzed by the thought of making a mistake." He nudged her closer with another press of his fingers and she obeyed his lead without seeming to notice. "Besides," he told her, "I'm never wrong."

"Ever?" Though he hadn't meant the claim in jest, she obviously took it that way. "I never suspected you'd be both decisive *and* infallible. However do you manage to keep that massive ego of yours in check?"

Staring down at her teasing smile and realizing this was the most relaxed he'd ever seen her, Kyros felt a rush of triumph. He'd found a chink in her armor. He'd scratched beneath her carefully guarded surface, and knowing that she'd lowered her guard, no matter how incrementally, arrowed through him with a sharp stab of arousal. Awash with the desire to kiss her again, to lose himself in the sweet recesses of her mouth and feel the staccato beat of her breath against his cheek, he lost the rhythm of the steps and stalled.

Laura, unprepared for his abrupt stop, continued on, stumbling over her own feet. A small sound of distress came from her throat, and her fingers gripped his shirt as she strove to regain her balance. "Sorry," she blurted as she pressed against his upper arm with her other hand. "I didn't expect you to—"

He turned to steady her, muttering an apology. The movement, combined with her own efforts, brought her flush up against legs and torso. The press of her small body, despite its modest layers of brown wool and silk, sent his pulse into a wild, careening rhythm. He ordered his hands to release her, to abandon the sweet curve of her narrow shoulders and back, but his body had an agenda of its own. Before he thought to stop it, his grip had tightened, hauling her up hard against him.

Her hands splayed high against his chest, trembling

just enough for him to divine her response to his nearness. Everything within him tightened as she stared up at him without breathing, her cheeks pink with agitation and her eyes wide with guilt. He waited for her to struggle within his arms, to call a halt to the madness that flared between them, but she was achingly, tellingly silent. The dark fan of her lashes fluttered and then rose, exposing her shocked, guilty gaze. Frozen in that searing moment of awareness, he recognized in her the same fascination that haunted his days and tortured his nights.

Theos.

She averted her eyes, her body radiating her unspoken desire while her warm breath buffeted his chest and chin. His muscles tensed and his throat thickened, overwhelmed by the desire to pull her up to his plundering, greedy mouth. He waited for her to move, either to withdraw or nudge him closer in wordless encouragement. Suspended in breathless anticipation, he watched her for any sign that she might want him enough to admit what was happening between them. But she didn't move at all, her trembling limbs motionless beneath his ravenous gaze.

Not trusting his own tenuous control with her pressed so intimately against him, he lifted his arms from her and took two agonized steps away. His mouth felt dry. His eyes refused to blink. He wondered if Laura knew how dangerous her position was. Two steps, less than a second, and he could snatch her up. He could carry her off to that big, white bed that had been driving him to madness and show her all the ways he could pleasure her.

But he'd be damned if he'd be the only one to succumb to the desire that simmered between them. He'd be damned if *he'd* be the one to beg. He'd never begged for anyone's attention or approval. He wasn't about to start now.

Not with her.

He wanted Laura weak with wanting for him, not the

other way around. He wanted to be the one in control, the one with all the power.

Then find someone who'll give it to you. Tonight. The cold, calculating voice reminded him that even though he couldn't get what he wanted from Laura, there was nothing stopping him from claiming it with someone else. Someone who would welcome him between her thighs and confide all her secrets in a desperate bid for intimacy.

"Thank you for the lesson," Laura said, her blue gaze avoiding his. "It's a relief to know I won't make an utter fool of myself tomorrow night."

Kyros forced a grim smile to his dry mouth and nodded curtly. "*Giagiá* will be pleased."

"I'll leave you to your work, then," she told him as she backed toward the door. "Until dinner?" she said by way of farewell.

"You'll have to eat without me," he said, "I need to spend the evening in the city. For business. You'll tell *Giagiá* for me?"

A flare of surprise flickered in her eyes, but she masked it with a quick nod. "Of course."

He wondered how she would react if she knew his reason for leaving had nothing to do with business and everything to do with finding a woman for the night. She'd undoubtedly disapprove. But he didn't care.

He didn't.

Laura slowly navigated the long hallways, returning to Titus's room as she tried to divert her thoughts from the vision of dancing with Kyros. She kept seeing herself pressed up against his side, their bodies moving in unison around the mirrored ballroom while Greek music swelled around them.

Being tutored by him, learning that she had the ability to dance when she'd never thought to court such humiliation again, had released a part of her she hadn't realized she'd

kept tamped down. It unsettled her, piquing her senses and making her feel anxious and troubled and nervous all at the same time. What else had she refused to try simply because she was afraid of failing? The question disturbed her, calling up deep-buried resentments she hadn't thought about in a long, long time.

She was glad Kyros had left for the night. The way he'd looked at her when she was in his arms, the way she'd wanted him to kiss her, had made her realize that being close to him was far too dangerous.

What would she have done, had he dipped his mouth to hers? Would she have remembered her vow to herself and then pushed him away? Or would she have welcomed him? The fact that her mind wavered between the two frightened her. Kyros had awakened something primal deep within her, a part of her psyche she didn't want to bring into the light of day.

She should feel nothing for her sister's husband beyond sympathy and friendship. But instead, she felt impossibly attracted to him. He didn't treat her as if she were merely an appendage to her more flashy twin, nor did he seem to be intimidated by the walls she'd erected between herself and the world.

He provoked her.

He teased her.

He talked to her as if he cared what she thought, he pushed her beyond her comfort zone, and he didn't allow her to retreat back into her comfortable shell. He treated her as if she were a woman. He made her feel alive. Vital. Free. And desires she'd never had to grapple with before now strained beneath the surface of her skin.

Breathing shakily, Laura dropped her face into her hands. Despite her vows to the contrary, she was coming to realize that she was not as strong as she thought she should be.

Being with Kyros eroded her will. He made her weak, and the admission frightened her.

The following morning, Laura overslept. Worrying that she'd failed to hear Titus's cries, she hurried to his room to find Kyros sitting in the rocking chair, his son comfortably nestled in the crook of his arm and drinking contentedly from his morning bottle.

"When did you get back?" she asked in surprise, her hand rising to clasp her robe closed over her unbound breasts and the thin T-shirt she'd worn to her solitary bed.

His eyes remained steadfastly on her face, though a sparking awareness of her relative state of undress simmered between them. "Two hours ago."

Startled, she squinted out at the late morning sunlight. "What time is it?"

"About ten."

"Ten?" Her free hand flew to her disheveled braid while worry about her rumpled appearance winnowed through her. "Why didn't you wake me up?"

"You looked like you needed your sleep."

The thought of him watching her sleep brought a sweet quake of familiarity to her limbs. She should have recoiled at the inappropriate intimacy of it, but she could not quite muster the will to push the swell of pleasure his words brought to her body. "I never sleep past six. I don't know why I did today."

"I'm sure it's six somewhere in the world." He made the observation the way he always did, as if her concerns needed only to be reframed to be dismissed.

Feeling nervous, aroused and awkward, she wrapped her free arm around her ribs and edged her way back to the adjoining door. "Even so, I don't feel any less lazy."

His gaze trailed leisurely over her dishabille, a small smile

playing about his mobile mouth. "It's a nice change from your usual efficient and buttoned-up self, if you ask me."

Embarrassed, she withdrew even further. "If you don't mind watching Titus for a little longer, I'll take just a minute to get dressed for the day."

"Take as long as you need." His eyes darkened while his voice retained its facetious timbre. "I'm in no rush."

She swallowed, and then ducked behind the door to close it between them. Nervous that there was no lock to bar him from the room, she rushed to change her clothes, brush her teeth and wash her face. She was in the middle of repairing her hair when the door to Titus's room opened and Kyros entered the gold suite.

"You get ready faster than any woman I've met." He came up behind her, his teasing green eyes finding hers in the large oval mirror. "Don't you know you're supposed to take at least an hour just to choose a pair of shoes?"

Flushing, she averted her eyes and reached for her hairpins. "I've never been one for primping."

"Why?" he asked her downturned head.

She didn't bother answering. She didn't primp because she didn't *want* to primp. What would be the point?

"You should try it sometime," he told her. "Maybe, like dancing, you'll discover you have a talent for it."

"It's a waste of time," she told him, her fingers fumbling with her hair as she grappled for composure. The slippery strands of black escaped her fingers and tumbled over her shoulders, a coiled mass she quickly reached to reclaim. "And there are other things I prefer to spend my time doing."

He didn't answer as she expected, instead stepping closer to stall her hands with his. Confused and exquisitely aware of how close he stood, she glanced up at his reflection as he slowly pulled her hands out to her sides.

Startled by the warm, tingling contact of his hands, Laura found she couldn't breathe as his heated gaze slid down the

disheveled tresses that had fallen over her chest. The dark strands, shot through with sunlight, parted over her breasts and fell in thick, twisted coils to her ribs. Her face burning with embarrassment, she tugged against his gentle grip, trying to free her wrists from his fingers. "Kyros. Please...I need to..."

Suddenly, he freed her, not moving as she twisted away from him and the mirror. But as she withdrew farther into the room, reaching with clumsy fingers to gather her hair, he merely followed.

Swallowing against a throat gone dry, she cast about for a topic of conversation to break the tension that had flared between them. "How was your trip to the city?" she asked in a thin voice as she twisted her hair at her nape. "I assume you averted whatever business crisis loomed?"

"Yes."

"Your grandmother missed you. She made a point of cooking your f-favorite meal—"

"I'm sure you kept her entertained."

"I did. But—" She stopped as her back collided with the bedpost. "Kyros," she whispered as her hands fell to grip the bedpost at her waist and her hair unfurled yet again.

He remained silent, the cadence of his breath faster than she remembered it being. But perhaps it was her own breathing that had become so fractured. Perhaps it was her own heightened awareness that made her misinterpret the hot gleam in his emerald eyes.

"I've never seen your hair down before."

"It's just hair," she mumbled, aware that her voice and hands were trembling. She tried to quell their quaking. "Hair I've been too busy to cut and—"

"Stop talking." Kyros's hands lifted to the sides of her neck and then he threaded his fingers along her scalp, drawing out the strands until they slipped to her shoulders and chest. "Just for a minute." He collected a single lock of hair and pressed it

to his mouth. Closing his eyes, he drew in a deep breath and then simply stood in silence. After a few seconds, a shudder traveled through him and then he dragged his eyes open to stare down at the shining strand entwined in his fingers.

Laura couldn't breathe. She couldn't even think.

Her hands flexed against the wooden post at her back, trembling with the desire to reach for him and drag his body closer. Confused by the warring factions of her brain and heart, she waited in agony for his lips to lower to hers, a silent plea for him to kiss her spiraling through her thoughts. *Please...I want you to...*

"I brought you some breakfast." Iona's entry shattered the silence and ratcheted Laura's attention away from Kyros's mouth. "Oh...I am sorry," she said as her green gaze skipped over the telling scene. "I did not mean to interrupt."

"It's no bother," Laura assured her as she ducked beneath Kyros's uplifted arm, a guilty blend of relief and frustration making her voice sound strained. "I was just heading to the kitchen."

"When you missed breakfast, I thought perhaps you were feeling ill."

"N-no. I just overslept," she said. Though Kyros hadn't protested her escape, she could feel the burning weight of his regard against her profile. Refusing to look at him, she strode forward to collect the small tray Iona had balanced on the arms of her wheelchair. "I forgot to set my alarm and Kyros didn't wake me up."

"I am glad," Iona said as she watched Laura deposit the tray on the white dressing table. "Every wife deserves to be spoiled by her husband on occasion."

"Perhaps," she agreed on a shaky laugh before she changed the subject and drew Iona into a discussion about the day's plans. She did *not* need to be daydreaming about a lifetime of being spoiled by Kyros.

CHAPTER TEN

When New Year's Eve arrived, Laura dressed for the party with a tangle of mixed feelings. Tonight would be her last night in Iona's gracious company, the last night of her role as Kyros's wife.

She was glad her deception was drawing to an end.

Wasn't she?

When Kyros came to collect her, his broad shoulders encased in tailored black and his blue-black hair gleaming, she found it difficult to remain visibly unaffected. Though Laura had always found Kyros to be disturbingly handsome, seeing him in his formal tuxedo of black and white…well, it stole her breath away.

With his groomed hair and polished shoes, he looked like a prince from a fairy tale, capable of slaying dragons and rescuing an entire legion of damsels in distress. Yet beneath the polish, a piratical gleam glimmered, hinting at his less-than-royal ascent to the upper ranks of society. It tugged at her, drawing her closer and making her mouth go dry.

Kyros's steps stalled as he looked down at her, and his emerald gaze skimmed over her dress and hair with deliberate slowness.

Knowing he'd expected her to dress for the festivities, she'd swallowed her misgivings and finally chosen a dress from the clothing Kyros had purchased for her. She'd had to

dig through all six suitcases to find it, but she'd unearthed a modest dress of black that seemed to be made of silk and smoke. The luxurious fabric skimmed her curves in a way that made her blush, so she'd mined the collection of designer clothing for a jacket that she could layer over it. The black jacket was a masterpiece of embroidery, its glittering onyx and silver beading a gorgeous complement to the dress she'd chosen.

She'd arranged her hair in its customary style, but she'd pulled a few strands down to curl against her cheeks and neck. She'd even dared to put a touch of pale pink on her lips. Dressed and coiffed as she was, she felt conspicuously feminine and exposed. And given the fact that she'd actually taken time to primp, she waited with bated breath for Kyros's reaction.

Her heart beating in anticipation, she stared into Kyros's inscrutable face as he slowly dragged his gaze back to hers.

"*That's* what you're going to wear to our wedding reception?"

Disappointment flared deep in her belly. "Yes."

"It's black."

A sudden stab of defensiveness sharpened her tone. "So? My choices were rather limited, and this was the best I could find."

"The best you could find?" he repeated. "After the fortune I spent on clothing for you, I'm confident there was something better in the bags I had packed for you."

"There wasn't," she snapped. "Unless, of course, you'd prefer I wear my navy suit."

He glared at her, his jaw ticking with disapproval. "No," he growled. "I would not prefer the navy suit."

Smarting under his obvious rejection of her efforts, she felt her temper flicker to life. "No? Then perhaps you should tell me which of those outrageous outfits you expected me to wear."

"I couldn't say, as I've not seen them. But I certainly didn't expect you to celebrate our union while dressed for a funeral."

Offended and hurt, Laura glared at him. "People wear black to parties all the time. And the beadwork makes it quite clear that I am celebrating. With you."

"It doesn't look like you're celebrating," he said dryly. "It looks like you're preparing for a dirge."

"I don't know why I even bothered to try to please you," she accused. "You're irrational and impossible."

"*I'm* irrational?" he repeated. "*You're* the woman too scared to step out of her shell because her dead sister once laughed at her."

She felt her face blanch. "What did you just say?"

"You heard me," he said in a low, flat voice. "You're scared."

She gasped. "I am not!"

"You hide behind nondescript clothing that does nothing for you just so you won't have to risk being compared to your sister."

Her mouth dropped open as her anger flared, sharp and hot.

"Admit it," he goaded. "Every decision you make is an effort to differentiate yourself from her, and I, for one, think it's time you stop letting her define who you are."

"The only one who compares me to Lana anymore is you!" No one had *ever* criticized her for her choices the way Kyros did. She was the *good* twin, the one who always made the right, selfless decision. How dare he imply otherwise?

"*Malakies.* You only see yourself through Lana's eyes, forgetting that her view of you was motivated by spite and selfishness."

"You have no idea what you're talking about!"

"Don't I? I know the truth is painful, but it doesn't have

to cripple you forever. You can still be the woman you were meant to be."

"The woman I was meant to be!" she repeated on a gasp.

"Yes. Lana did her best to kill whatever part of you that might have offered her any competition. She made you afraid to be a woman by convincing you that you'd fail. And you know what? You let her win."

"She didn't win anything!"

"Prove it, then," he returned. "Prove you can be a woman instead of some buttoned-up little bird who's too scared to let the world see who she really wants to be."

"*This* is who I want to be," she sputtered, more furious than she could ever remember being. "And the only reason you don't like it is because you've never known a decent woman in your life!"

He shrugged while his eyes continued to bore into hers. "Tell that to yourself all you want. I recognize a repressed, frightened woman when I see one."

"You think *I'm* repressed and frightened?" she shrieked, her anger sending a hot, crimson wave of rage to her face. "You, who can't see women as anything but objects to manipulate, think *I'm* frightened?" She wanted to smack him, to hurt him the way he had hurt her, but she couldn't come up with an accusation that would wound him deeply enough.

"Yes," he said while cool satisfaction simmered deep in his green eyes.

"Well, you're wrong. I'm not frightened. Not of you, not of this stupid party, and certainly not of being myself."

"You're lying. It took me a while to figure it out, but now I see it. You're terrified of going after what you want."

"What I want?" she scoffed. "You have no idea what I want. And just because I refuse to bully and lie my way into getting it doesn't make me a coward."

"Doesn't it?"

"No. It takes *far* more courage to behave honorably, to

draw a line and not cross it, than it does to manipulate the truth to your own ends," she accused, her voice trembling with rage. "And the fact that you can't see that? Well, it makes me pity you. *You're* the one who lies to your own grandmother and married a woman you couldn't stand. *You're* the one who's afraid to see the painful truth about the relationships you have with the people you're supposed to love."

Livid and shaking, she stomped back to the closet and ripped open Lana's suitcases, one after the other, until the closet was littered with extravagant fabric and colors of every hue. "But if you want me to dress like Lana, God forbid I defy you! You've blackmailed me into playing her part, so I'll do it without complaint. But don't you *dare* imply that pretending to be the woman you want is the same as being the woman *I* want to be."

Kyros watched her in stunned silence as she glared at him, regretting the harsh words he'd been unable to withhold. Why had he behaved like such a bastard, when it was obvious she'd taken such pains to please him? She *did* look pretty and primped, her hair looser than usual and her slim body's curves subtly highlighted by the wispy diagonal design of her black dress.

When he'd first seen her, his body had leapt the same way as always, and the thought of squiring her about on his arm had actually brought a rush of pleasure…until he realized she'd done everything possible to conceal herself beneath the finery he'd purchased.

Seeing her hiding beneath her clothes, her torso and arms covered, had ignited a flare of irritation he hadn't expected to feel. So he'd lashed out, taking a stab at what he now suspected were her true motives. He'd accused her of succumbing to her sister's poisonous influence, and judging by her unfiltered reaction, he'd stumbled on the truth at last. She didn't hide because she wanted to keep him on edge. She hid because she was afraid. She hid because she'd been hurt.

And like a total bastard, he'd hurt her again.

Knowing he'd lashed out at her when she deserved so much better from him lodged an uncomfortable knot of regret deep within his chest. A strange, sick feeling swamped him. He felt cold. Bleak. And afraid that by baiting her the way he had, he'd pushed her into hating him.

"I'm sorry," he said in a thick voice. "You're right." Pausing, he realized he wanted things back the way they were. He didn't want her hurting. Not because of him. "*Theos.* I've been an ass. Wear whatever you want."

"You can't recant your words now," she said, her arms bunched tightly around her ribs. "I already know your opinion."

"My opinion doesn't matter, and I exaggerated anyway." He felt as if he'd locked his feet in ice, and the coldness crept with stealthy insistence toward every cell. "You look beautiful."

"No. You're right. I agreed to play the part of Lana. I even signed a contract to that effect. And we both know I've been shirking my duty. I've been myself instead of her, and I should have known that being me would never suffice."

"That's not what I—"

"Enough." She turned to face him with a set jaw and flashing eyes. "Tell me what you would have me wear, and I'll wear it," she said curtly as she gestured to the jumbled array of designer clothing. "Do you want me in red? Blue? A pale green to match your eyes?"

He swallowed uneasily, his libido immediately triggered by the thought of her flushed torso and the swells of her rounded breasts no longer hidden by nondescript browns and grays. "Laura—"

"Red. That's what Lana would wear, isn't it?" She dipped to snag a sleeveless red dress the color of blood and shook it out between them. "Will this suffice? Will it make me enough like a *woman* to suit your taste?"

When he didn't answer, his tongue thick and his mouth too dry to accommodate speech, she stomped past him to the bathroom and slammed the door.

Safely ensconced in the tiled bathroom of white and gold, Laura jerked at her black jacket and dress with angry, determined yanks. He wanted her to look like Lana? Well, she'd show him Lana. She'd look so much like her sister, he'd be sorry he ever asked her to change. Stripped down to her white slip and bra, she reached for the structured gown of velvet and sequins. After stepping into the shaped torso and then tugging it up over her ribs, it became evident that her white underthings would never work with the plunging neckline of the dress.

Realizing she would have to go without a bra sent a hot tide of embarrassment flooding from head to toe, until even her breasts were flushed a scorching pink. But she couldn't back down now. Not after the way she'd flung Kyros's accusations back in his face. Resolute, she reached to shed her slip and bra. She shimmied the formfitting dress over her curves and fought the second thoughts that swamped her as she struggled with the zipper.

When she finally managed to fasten the top clasp between her shoulder blades, she bent at the waist to release the pins from her hair. She finger-combed out the long waves, shaking her head and then flinging the heavy mass up and over her shoulders. The view of her profile in the mirror startled her, the rich red of the gown contrasting sharply with her pale skin and dark hair.

She turned to examine the shapely silhouette the formfitting gown created, the flash of cleavage and snowy breast revealed by its cut making her feel entirely out of her element. Dressed in the gown Kyros had chosen, she looked bold. Confident. And undeniably feminine.

It made her feel vulnerable. Exposed. And strangely,

wildly powerful. It was a dress she never would have chosen for herself, a dress she would have never dared to wear.

And yet, with Kyros, she dared.

It was a heady, dizzying, frightening realization. It sent her pulse into a flurried, uneven beat, and thinned her breath.

It's just an act. It doesn't mean you've changed. You're still you.

"I'm still me," she murmured before she braced her shoulders and reached for the door handle.

Kyros stood uneasily in their suite, staring at the door and berating himself for not leaving well enough alone. But then the doorknob turned and the door swung open to reveal his wildest fantasies brought to life. Kyros locked his knees to keep them from buckling, his eyes greedily taking in every detail of Laura's stunning transformation.

His ravenous gaze couldn't decide where to alight: the shadowed cleavage between her high, white breasts, the long, pale line of her bare throat and arms, the notch of her tiny waist, or the wild tumble of her dark hair.

He couldn't breathe, and his chest felt too small to contain the beating heart within. He had never seen a woman so stunningly, naturally gorgeous in his entire life. The cold numbness that had claimed his lungs dissolved in a flare of liquid heat, his control thinning to a tenuous thread as she hitched her chin and met his eyes.

"I trust this will suffice?" she challenged in a crisp voice.

He stared into her icy blue eyes and nodded silently. She hadn't forgiven him, that much was clear. Perhaps this was her vengeance. And if it was, he had to concede defeat: he had no desire to fight with her anymore.

Seeing her in all her feminine splendor brought a physical ache so intense he hurt. He burned to touch her, to explore her soft white curves with his body and lips and hands. He wanted to taste her skin, to bury his fingers in her hair and

tip her throat to his ravenous mouth. Their suite's big, square bed taunted him, reminding him of how futile his desire was.

"Laura," he started. "What I said earlier… I'm sorry. Just because you don't choose to put yourself on display for the world to see does not mean that you—"

"I know," she responded tartly. "But this isn't about me. It's about *your* party, *your* grandmother and *your* wife I'm supposed to imitating. So for the time being, I shall have to overlook your rude behavior and simply accept my lot for the evening."

Feeling chastened, Kyros merely nodded his head in agreement.

"Shall we?" she said archly, her hips moving in a seductive sway as she strode toward the door.

Watching her legs move beneath the curve-skimming shell of red distracted him, filling his mind with visions of her writhing, arching limbs beneath his sheets. An erotic image of him catching her from behind, pulling her up hard against his aroused flesh and burying his face against the side of her scented neck filled his mind's eye, bringing a flush of perspiration and a swell of longing to his groin.

He wanted to fill his hands with her soft breasts, to lift her, spread her and then bury himself deep inside her welcoming heat. Wanting her and knowing she'd never accept him tweaked the back of his neck and made his muscles bunch.

You brought this on yourself, he thought with an undeniable stab of realization. *You deserve to suffer the consequences.*

CHAPTER ELEVEN

THEY ARRIVED late to the party and found that Iona and her staff had created magic within the spacious ballroom. White lights fanned out from the chandeliers to the window casings, forming a glittering canopy over the milling crowd of guests. Along the perimeter of the room, long tables groaned under a feast fit for kings, while the open bars at three corners promised a night of unsurpassed revelry.

For several seconds, she and Kyros stood unnoticed, Laura feeling dazed by the spectacular display of flowers, light and polished marble. There were more people in the ballroom than she'd thought it capable of holding, some already gathering in the center of the dance floor while others staked out chairs and tables.

But then someone caught sight of Kyros, and news of his arrival spread through the crowd like flames among tinder. A roar of welcome rose from the room, followed by a swell of outstretched arms and grinning faces as she and Kyros were absorbed into the crowd.

Amid a flurry of introductions and clapped shoulders, Laura learned that the guests originated from all parts of Kyros's life. There were childhood friends from the servant ranks, schoolmates, college buddies and business acquaintances. There were men who'd shared boyhood antics and the women who'd married them, good-natured rivals who'd

later become allies and grateful families who owed their livelihood to Kyros's generosity and support.

Everywhere she looked, smiling friends were waiting to raise a toast in Kyros's direction, their obvious happiness in his good fortune bringing genuine pleasure to their celebration. Watching them, she realized that Kyros, despite his claims of ruthless bullying, was beloved by all who knew him.

It suddenly made her feel petty and small for fighting with him. And she realized that he'd been right about her. She had chosen the modest black dress for exactly the reason he had accused her of. Yes, it had been elegant and beautiful, but she'd known it would allow her to blend in and become invisible in the way she preferred.

She'd been nervous about claiming a place at Kyros's side, about publicly assuming a role she'd never be fit to fill. Dressing the way she had was her way of reminding herself of the boundaries she needed to maintain. There were already too many instances of her forgetting her place, her role and the fact that none of what they shared was real. It was becoming too easy to imagine the two of them together, building a life and being parents to Titus as if he belonged to the two of them.

But this week was not her life. It never could be.

"Attention, please," Iona's clear voice announced as she tapped a microphone that had been set up for the band. "Attention!"

The crowd settled and turned as one to listen to their hostess as she lifted a glass of wine.

"Thank you all for coming to celebrate the wedding of my dear grandson and his bride. Kyros, I am proud of you for finally having the good sense to settle down with such a delightful woman. Lana, welcome to the family. And to the rest of you, please eat, dance and enjoy yourselves as we embrace the New Year together."

An uproarious cheer accompanied her toast, settling to a good-natured hum as the guests turned to load their plates high for their celebratory meal.

Kyros escorted Laura to the place of honor nearest the curved wall of window and mirrors, and in between bites of dinner and sips of wine, she and Kyros conversed with a steady stream of guests who stopped by to reminisce and reconnect before the dancing began.

It felt very much like a typical wedding receiving line, where Kyros introduced her to old acquaintances and then exchanged brief updates on family, friends and business before the next guest cycled through. By the time Laura had finished her meal, her face ached from smiling.

"If everyone can take their places for the serving of the cake," said Iona, who'd reclaimed her place at the microphone, "we shall see who will have the best luck in the coming year."

Kyros leaned to slice into the fragrant *vasilopita* cake the circulating wait staff had delivered to their table, his green eyes teasing hers as he asked, "Did *Giagiá* tell you whoever finds the coin in their piece gets good luck for the year?"

Laura nodded. "She made me put extras in ours," she confided in a low whisper. "She thinks if we *both* find a coin, Titus will have a sibling before the new year is out."

Kyros grinned, making a display of sliding first her slice and then his onto their plates. "Then here's to *Giagiá*'s machinations."

It took less than three forkfuls of the almond-encrusted confection before Laura discovered a coin wrapped in cellophane. She held hers up in triumph, reveling in her find until Kyros dug his out of his cake and held it aloft as well. Laughing, Laura realized she hadn't experienced such a lovely New Years Eve in…well…ever.

"Are you ready to dance?" Kyros asked once all the guests

had finished their desserts and the musicians had resumed their seats at their instruments.

"It's now or never, isn't it?" She accepted his outstretched fingers and allowed him to escort her to the center of the dance floor, where they were immediately drawn into a large circle of inebriated guests. Soon, looped arms closed the circle and the musicians launched into the familiar *kalamatian* tune.

They danced, circling right, then left, then right again, as everyone whooped and stomped. Jackets were shed, shirtsleeves were rolled up and wine was consumed in generous portions until someone hollered that the fireworks were starting.

Everyone surged outside, packing shoulder-to-shoulder on the wide patio overlooking the sea. A rocket was launched, joining the stars in a flurry of white sparks. One flare after another filled the night sky, accompanied by a chorus of appreciative gasps and a hint of sulfurous smoke.

Laura felt Kyros's warmth at her back, and his long arms looped low around her hips as they stared up at the sky together. It should have bothered her, how right it felt to stand within his arms.

But it didn't.

She pushed her niggling conscience aside and decided to enjoy the moment while it lasted. They were surrounded by good people who believed they were celebrating Kyros's union to her. They didn't need to know they'd been lied to.

Laura had agreed to play a role. She owed it to them all to play it well. So she leaned back against Kyros's wide chest, savoring his heat and the weight of his hands against her abdomen.

"Ten...nine...eight..."

She and Kyros joined the raucous countdown while the last firework exploded across the sky. And when the stroke of midnight chimed, she didn't protest when Kyros slowly

turned her within his arms and dipped his head to hers. Beneath her buzzing awareness of his hot, hot mouth plundering hers with mind-numbing skill, she became aware of a riotous cheering. Before she could contain her reaction to his kiss, he'd straightened and then turned to grin out at the whooping crowd.

"Happy New Year!" he called.

"Happy New Year!" his friends shouted back.

Caught up on a tide of well-wishes, Laura found herself swept back inside for another round of dancing. After half an hour of nonstop revelry, Laura was ready for a few moments of respite. Warm from her exertions, she took advantage of a pause between songs to search out some fresh air.

She opted for the far exit, hoping that it would prove to be less crowded. The tall glass door led out onto the large granite terrace, its periphery surrounded by graceful urns, potted evergreens and statuary she hadn't noticed before.

Between two prickly junipers she found a shallow series of steps leading to a steep rock overhang and a railing overlooking the sea. Its dizzying position over the water far, far below made her feel as if she'd stumbled into Poseidon's realm.

Leaning against the cold railing, she stared down at the sea while shafts of moonlight cast her exposed arms in a pale glow. Shivering and yet savoring the chill, she straightened to rub her hands over her bare skin.

"It's too cold to be out here in that dress."

Startled, Laura turned to find Kyros had followed her outside. She smiled up at him and hugged her arms a little tighter. "I wasn't cold until now."

He moved down the remaining steps, closing the space between them as he came to stand next to her. "Would you like me to warm you up?"

"What?" she asked, her pulse suddenly clamoring within her ears.

He removed his jacket and then draped it over her shoul-

ders. Its warmth, Kyros's warmth, felt as intimate as a touch, and she felt heat flare along the surface of her skin.

"Everybody's probably wondering where you are," she stammered as she abandoned the railing and started toward the ballroom.

He caught her before she'd made it two steps, his big hand gripping the back of her arm and slowly turning her around to face him. "Don't go," he said quietly. "Stay."

She swallowed, her entire body going still. Being out here, with the magical night closing around the two of them, was not safe. Her brain knew it. Her heart knew it. But she couldn't seem to make her body move.

"I've been thinking about what you said earlier," he said, his grip softening to a caress. "About how I'm afraid to see the truth."

"Don't," she said, pulling free of his touch and retreating another couple of steps. "I was angry and I was lashing out. Your fears, if you even have any, are none of my business."

He followed her with undeniable intent. "What if I want to make it your business?"

She lifted a hand to where he'd touched her, rubbing the spot that still tingled with the impression of his long fingers. "You don't."

"Why wouldn't I?"

When she didn't answer, Kyros stepped closer to admit the damning realization that had plagued his brain ever since their argument. "You're right about me, you know. I accused you of hiding, of being afraid, when I should have looked in a mirror first."

She shook her head and backed away from him, her fingers fluttering up to her throat. "Kyros. Don't. It's over. We don't have to talk about it."

"Damn it, Laura," he corrected, with gravel in his voice. "I'm trying to apologize here, trying to make things right, and you're putting up walls again."

"I have to," she said. "To do otherwise just complicates things."

"So what if things get a little complicated?"

"I don't want things complicated. Once this night is over and you're thinking rationally, you'll agree with me."

"I am thinking rationally. Probably for the first time in my life."

"No," she insisted. "You're not. You're frustrated because you've been trying to seduce me for the entire week and it's not working. It's compromising your ability to think clearly." She must have realized what she'd just said, because her eyes turned into glittering pools of dismay. She pressed her mouth into a firm line, as if to keep it from spilling out more inconvenient truths.

"Damn right it is." He may as well admit it, as fighting it wasn't getting him anywhere. "Anybody who sees me can tell I burn for you. It's no secret I want you in my bed, squirming with pleasure beneath me. And the hell of it is, you're the first woman I *haven't* seduced, because the challenge of chipping beneath your shell intrigued me more than getting into your bed."

Her eyes, wide enough to fall into, flitted from his in obvious distress. "Kyros, I don't have any shell. I'm just—"

"You're wrong," he interrupted. "You have more armor than any woman I've met. And I want to understand why. Tonight, I scratched the surface. I *saw* you, and I don't want to stop until I know everything. All of it. Don't you realize that?" He felt his body tense with the admission, the desire that had tormented him from the first time he'd seen her making his muscles go rigid with unmet, frustrated arousal. "If it were just an issue of my libido, I'd have taken my ease with another woman days ago. But I didn't. I couldn't, even though I tried. And you want to know why? Because I've discovered that I respect you more than I've ever respected another woman." He shook his head and stepped closer to

her, reaching for her small, narrow hands. "And the fact that
I've just admitted that to Lana's twin sister unnerves me as
much as it does you. Believe me. But since we're talking truth
here, I thought you should hear *my* version."

His confession clearly distressed Laura, as she yanked
her hands free and backed away from him in small, stumbling steps.

"Wait." He caught her and then swung her into a small
cove of privacy between two large potted plants and a statue
of Aphrodite. "Don't run away from this."

"I have to," she said, her abbreviated breathing making
her voice hitch. "You're talking crazy."

"You can't dare me to face the truth and then run away
when I do."

"This isn't the truth," she told him as she tugged free of
his grip and sought shelter in the small bower formed by
Aphrodite's thigh and a potted Greek juniper. "You're just
reacting to this dress, to the lie you want your grandmother
to believe, and to an entire room of people thinking we're
married. Throw in a bottle of ouzo and some fireworks, and
the night's bound to get crazy."

"It's not just this night, Laura. I've wanted you since I first
saw you in New York."

She gave a dismissive little bleat of a laugh. "In your bed,
maybe, but that's it. Don't try to make this about anything
more than frustrated lust."

"I don't deny the lust. *Theos,* I'd be a fool to claim I don't
want you that way. But it's more than lust. I know that now
because I can *see* you. You may not want me to, but I do. And
I want to see more. I want to *know* you." When she might
have protested, he talked over her, ticking off her traits like
a child reciting his sums. "I know you're generous. You're
kind. You value family as much as I do, and you'd do anything to make those you love happy."

"Anyone would—"

"But you also have a battle going on deep inside you, a battle between who you are and who you think you should be. At first, I thought you were hiding because you were as manipulative as your sister. I thought your sweetness was a weapon you'd sharpened to a fine, cutting edge. But I was wrong. Your sweetness is real, and what you're hiding is the person you won't allow yourself to be. You're hiding, not because you want to manipulate me, but because you're afraid to want anything that Lana claimed for herself. You're afraid to want *me* because Lana wanted me first."

Her whole body froze, her mouth dropping open to emit a single, soft gasp.

"Admit it," he challenged her. "Admit you want me as much as I want you."

"No," she whispered while her face turned white. "Wanting you…it's not right and I won't do it. I can't."

"How can it be wrong?" he urged, stepping close enough that her only escape would be into the spiny arms of the evergreen. "When the feel of you between my hands, when the taste of your mouth and the scent of your skin—"

"Stop," she begged, her splayed hand rising to halt his forward progress. "You don't know what you're—"

"I *do* know," he said as another step brought his chest flush with her outstretched hand. "I know how you look at me when you think I'm not watching. I know how you react when I'm close enough to kiss you. I see the way your breath goes shallow and your pupils dilate and your body reaches for mine."

Her gaze darted away from his and she pulled her hand back, knotting it at her waist. "It doesn't!"

"So if I kissed you again," he dared in a liquid voice as he inched even closer, "you'd push me away? You'd convince me in no uncertain terms that you don't want me?"

She kept her focus on the ground, though he could sense

her tension mount. "Yes, Kyros," she claimed unsteadily. "I'd push you away. I'd convince you once and for all that I—"

He reached for her, hauled her forward onto her toes until her chest collided with his and then lowered his mouth to hers.

CHAPTER TWELVE

A SMALL sound of distress gathered in Laura's throat as she went perfectly still, her body paralyzed by the storm of sensation sweeping through her veins. Kyros kissed her the way he had before, a raw, drugging possession so filled with erotic passion that she couldn't help but respond. She forgot about the party continuing on without them. She forgot about everything but his hot, dark mouth claiming hers.

His dark head blotted out the moonlight and his wide hands blotted out the cold. Every sense narrowed to the two of them, to the gentle, insistent sweeps of his lips and tongue as he slowly, inexorably eroded her will.

Every cell seemed to be on fire. And suddenly, she couldn't get close enough. She slid her hands from beneath the tuxedo jacket he'd draped over her, finding his wide, warm chest and the bellows of his ribs beneath cool cotton. Inhaling greedily, she tried to draw more of his scent, heated by dance and arousal, deep into her lungs.

Shaken, wanting and awash with sensations too fractured to catalogue, she dragged her mouth from his and pressed her forehead against the row of black buttons fastening his shirt. Breathing in choppy gusts, she clutched his muscled back while trying to gather her senses.

"Laura," he groaned, sounding as undone as she. "Don't hide from me...don't tell me this is wrong." His hand lifted

to her nape, threading through her hair to the scalp beneath before he tilted her head back yet again. His lips sought hers anew, plundering in deep, searching forays that stole her breath.

Unable to fight him, she responded in kind, taking full advantage of this stolen moment in time to steep herself in his taste and texture and the heady excitement she'd waited a lifetime to feel.

She tasted ouzo on his tongue, felt the heat of his body beneath her splayed hands. She wanted to lick him, to feel his skin against hers, to wrap her limbs around him while he taught her all the things her body longed to know. Frustrated, she lifted to her toes and arched against him, reaching, yearning, unable to draw him close enough.

Sensing her distress, Kyros dipped to gather her up into his arms. Without breaking their kiss, he carried her to the far side of the patio and the relative privacy the dark side of the house provided. He found a stone bench nestled among a garden of hibernating foliage and settled into it, placing her across his lap while his mouth continued to ravage hers. One arm, as strong and tensile as steel, braced her back while his other hand explored her rib and hip in commanding strokes.

Pleasure winnowed sharply within her veins, bringing heat and a quivering, excited desire to touch him. She reached for his hard neck and the silky black hair at his nape, tugging him closer as she twisted and arched within his arms.

When her breasts brushed against his chest, he broke the kiss to bow over her, his hands flexing against her willing flesh. She felt his hot mouth track a trail of fire from her ear to the vulnerable curve of her neck, his tongue tasting the underside of her jaw and then the delicate arch of her collarbone. She shivered and squirmed, lifting to him, while his lips began their achingly slow descent toward the shadowed valley between her breasts.

Desperate for him to go faster, she felt her riotous pulse

gather and swell. It throbbed…everywhere. In her ears, in her fingertips, in the aching, tender tips of her contained breasts and in the untouched apex between her thighs. "Kyros," she whimpered, her legs shifting and her skirt becoming bunched between them.

"Shhh," he murmured as his fingers slid north to traverse the edge of her bodice. A series of subtle, deft tugs soon left her breasts free to the night air and his hot, hot gaze. Before she had a chance to protest, his searing mouth dipped low, pulling erotic sensation to every inch of her sensitized skin. She writhed up toward his searching lips, clutching his dark head between her hands as his tongue traced a delicate line around the perimeter of her nipple.

Her breath shuddered and then held, the exquisite weight of anticipation gathering everything up tight as the damp forays of lip and tongue circled slowly, slowly toward the tip of her breast. When his kiss finally, finally closed over her, she bucked beneath him, a small cry of pleasure escaping her throat.

Oh…she wanted to feel him…everywhere. Around her, inside her, over her. His big hand moved as if she'd spoken the thought aloud, his fingers tracking soft, seeking circles that started between her knees and slowly navigated upward. Her thighs parted of their own accord, urging him closer while her fingers dug into his scalp and her tongue twined with his. *Touch me. Touch me.*

He obliged with agonizing slowness, the tip of his thumb stroking softly over the patch of cotton between her legs. She arched beneath his seeking fingers and then gasped when he tugged the thin panel of fabric aside and found her opening. She closed her eyes against a burning blend of embarrassment and arousal, too focused on the magic of his fingers to do anything but pant against his marauding mouth.

His skill betrayed an intimate knowledge of feminine flesh, and she jolted beneath the gentle invasion of his hand.

Excruciatingly aware of his fingertips, the soft rasp of callus against sensitive, slick flesh, she whimpered as an involuntary tide of clenching pleasure rose, receded and rose again.

One finger entered her virginal flesh, stretching and stroking while her body throbbed and clung to accommodate the new sensation. "I want you," he breathed against her mouth.

"Yes…" Her hips moved in cadence with his hand, her body a slave to his talented touch.

"You want me, too," he murmured as his mouth slid from hers to her throat. He hitched her higher with his free arm, tilting her breasts to his lips and tongue. He tugged, nipped and scissored his teeth against the tender tips, his mouth moving in aching counterpoint to the rhythm of his hand.

Her ability to track his movements faltered in a swell of sensation, in a coil of clenching, spasming pleasure that rocketed through her spine and womb. She cried out, her entire body racked with tremors, and he silenced her with a deep, stroking kiss.

She clung to him, tears leaking from her eyes, and realized she wanted to touch every warm, browned inch of his big body and to have him touch her the same way. She wanted him inside her, plunging into her, branding her as his. She wanted it more than she wanted her next breath, more than she wanted honor or rightness or her self-respect.

And with the realization of her want came a torrent of fear. Because she knew that afterward, when their appetites had been sated and their passions spent, she would have nothing left.

"Kyros," she gasped, pushing against his shoulders with unsteady hands, "I'm sorry…I can't do this…please stop. Please."

His body grew still, his head still dipped over her and his rough palm cupping her sex. He slowly straightened and then skewered her with eyes of green flame. He continued

to stare at her as he removed his hand from beneath her skirt and then tugged her bodice back into respectability.

Once she was put back to rights, she struggled to abandon his lap. He hauled her back to press swift, branding kisses against her mouth until her protests evaporated into quiet moans of distress. He kissed her until she accepted that he wasn't done with her. "You're mine," he whispered into her damp, swollen, and unresisting mouth. "You may as well stop fighting it."

Stop fighting? She stared up at him, her heart drumming a terrified rhythm against her ribs, and then she lurched to her feet. She couldn't belong to him. He'd been Lana's and she'd spent her life not wanting the things her sister claimed. As much as she wanted him, she wasn't foolish enough to think she could ever, ever live her life with a man that had married her sister. She couldn't. She'd lose all sense of herself. She'd become another person entirely.

"I can't," she told him in a thin voice. "I can't do this and live with myself."

"Why?" he asked.

"We have to forget this happened," she told him, her heart clubbing against her throat. "It never happened."

"No," he said thickly. He launched up to reach for her, but she backed away from him, avoiding his touch.

"I want to stay involved in Titus's life, and I won't be able to if this continues."

"This has nothing to do with Titus," he countered, his big hands lifting to the sides of her jaw. He tipped her face, until she had no choice but to meet his searing gaze. "This has to do with us, Laura, and what you're trying to deny. You want me. And I want you." Raw need made his voice husky. "I want you with me, with Titus, as part of—"

"Stop," she beseeched him as she gripped his broad wrists, her own desire to succumb bringing a choking thickness to her throat. "Please stop. We have to pretend this never hap-

pened. And it can't ever happen again. Please. I couldn't bear it if I lost Titus, too."

He stared down at her in taut silence until he seemed to come to a decision. Exhaling unsteadily, he released her and slowly stepped away from her. "All right. I won't press to change your mind because I want you with Titus, as well. My son needs you in his life. We need you to stay."

She swallowed nervously, not sure how she'd manage with the temptation of having him so close and yet off-limits. But at the same time, the thought of helping to raise Titus, of loving him and holding him and watching him grow, trumped the mad desires of her body. She could restrain herself. She could redraw the lines between them. "I'll stay to nanny Titus, but you can't touch me again," she warned in a trembling voice.

"I wouldn't dream of it," he agreed, though his ravenous gaze told her otherwise. A tic in his jaw told her he'd clenched his teeth. "Actually," he amended, "that's a lie. I doubt I'll be dreaming of much else for a while yet."

"Kyros," she scolded softly while a fierce flush made her feel hot yet again.

"I will promise not to touch you," he said. "But I won't promise to control my dreams when they're the only respite remaining to me."

She couldn't continue to look at him with his green eyes boring into hers. So she backed away from him until she could escape him without appearing to run.

Kyros didn't return to the ballroom for several long minutes, taking advantage of the brisk, biting cold to cool the thwarted hunger that had strung his body as tight as a bowstring. Heavy, aching arousal tormented both his thoughts and his twitching muscles.

Kissing, touching and tasting Laura was no longer limited to fantasy. He *knew* her scent, her softness, the low sounds

she made in her throat as she squirmed against him. He knew the slick velvet of her feminine core, he knew the throb of her pulse against his fingers. He knew the passion she kept buttoned up beneath her brown suits and her infernal wall of fear.

He knew *her*.

Finally.

But he also knew she meant what she'd said. For some reason, she'd decided that being with him was wrong. And if he convinced her to dismantle the walls she'd built between them, she'd never forgive him. She'd never forgive herself.

She'd leave.

Could he survive the torment of having her close, but forever out of reach? To keep her in Titus's life, could he stay away from her?

What choice did he have?

When he finally returned to the celebration of their counterfeit marriage, his eyes immediately found her in the crowded room. He tore his gaze from her vivid red dress, forcing his mind from the feel of that velvet beneath his fingertips and the taste of her soft flesh beneath his tongue. He kept his attention on the dancers and the various acquaintances who approached him for words of investment advice or to exchange memories about a shared childhood prank. He laughed at their stories and offered his opinions whenever anyone solicited them. But through it all, his body, his mind and his very soul burned for Laura.

The ambition that had consumed him for decades, the desire to face every challenge, to prove his worth and to make up for his claim on his mother's young life were like a morning mist of dew when compared to the tsunami of want that Laura wrought in him. He didn't know how to contain it, how to direct it or corral it or control it.

But control it, he would. Because to do otherwise would be to lose her forever.

CHAPTER THIRTEEN

BY THE time the party wound down to its inevitable conclusion, Laura had consumed more than her fair share of wine and champagne. But it still hadn't settled her nerves.

Pretending that she wasn't aware of Kyros's every movement after he'd returned to the ballroom had been an exercise of willpower she hadn't known she possessed. Her every cell had hummed with awareness of his dark, brooding presence, with a poignant ache that contrasted sharply with the urgings of her own conscience. And now, with the last of the guests departed and a fatigued Iona already off to bed, the moment of reckoning had arrived.

She and Kyros had one more night to spend together as pseudo man and wife. One more night where she feigned sleep while Kyros's warm, steady breathing kept her burning and awake.

Kyros drew up alongside Laura, ushering her toward the ballroom doors. On the way out, he snagged a half-empty bottle of ouzo and two small glasses.

Once they made it back to their suite, Kyros poured them both a drink, tugged off his bowtie and jacket and then claimed the white sofa facing the fireplace. He drained his glass in a single swallow, then leaned to refill his drink before sitting back to stare at her. For a scalding moment, her eyes couldn't seem to abandon his.

Dark and malevolent and male, he'd unbuttoned his shirt, and the glimpse of hard chest and black hair sent a torrent of longing through her thoughts. She wanted to bury her fingers and mouth and nose against those springy curls. She wanted the rough texture of him against her aching breasts, the scent of him in her mouth.

"You can't sleep in that dress," he told her in a strained voice as he gestured toward the closet with his glass. "Change, and then you can join me for a drink."

She nodded wordlessly and then escaped to the closet. She felt his eyes following her, felt his burning regard against the line of her back and thigh. When she closed the door between them, she buried her face in her hands as she tried to gather her strength. *Make it through this night, and you'll be able to handle anything. You can nanny Titus without compromising everything you believe in.*

He was waiting for her when she emerged, and he'd lowered the lights and lit a fire. "Join me," he invited, holding up her glass of ouzo.

"I don't think that's a good idea," she said in a soft voice.

"Are you afraid?" he asked thickly as his gaze canvassed her protective armor of long-sleeved cotton shirt, sweater, flannel pajama pants and thick wool socks.

She licked her lips and stared at his chest. "Yes."

"Why?"

"I don't trust myself around you," she said carefully, her apprehension mounting as she lifted her gaze to his hooded expression. Dangerously attractive and intense, he posed a threat she didn't dare underestimate. "You make me feel things…think and do things…that I shouldn't."

"Who says you shouldn't?"

"I do."

"You—"

"No," she interrupted. "You told me you respected me, and it's because I try to behave honorably. I have always

worked to live my life above reproach and those efforts are what have made me the woman I am. They've made me into the woman you wish to have in Titus's life. But when I allow you too close, I'm tempted to forfeit my honor. I'm tempted to forfeit who I am. And that's—"

"*Theos,* the woman who wants to forfeit the chains of her constrictive code of honor *is* the woman I respect," he said roughly. "How can you not see that?"

She rubbed her forehead, closing her eyes against the wretched desire to believe him, to let him convince her that she was wrong.

"Laura." His voice was much closer, his ouzo-scented breath wafting across her cheek. "Why can't you just let yourself be happy? Why is it so wrong to let yourself *feel*?"

"Because—"

"Because it's wrong?" he interrupted. "Because you don't deserve to have the things that Lana took for granted and then threw away?"

She felt herself whiten at that. "I don't want the things Lana had. I never did. She—"

"I know. It's a character flaw to accept any hint of longing for what your sister had. But if you're going to deny yourself everything just because she claimed it first, at least have the courage to admit your motivation. Admit that you don't want a life with me because it was the life she threw away."

Reeling from surprise, she stared at his intent expression, sure she'd misinterpreted his words. "What do you mean, a life with you?"

"What do you think it means?" he asked. He lifted his hands to her upper arms. "This week has felt real to me in a way no other relationship has. Hasn't it felt real to you?" His fingers slid up, to the hasty twist of hair she'd knotted at her nape, and his palms cupped her jaw as he tilted her face to hers.

Her body trembled in helpless response. Unable to meet

his probing, knowing gaze, she closed her eyes while a whimper of distress and desire collected in her throat. She didn't want to respond to his touch this way. She didn't want the recesses of her body to quiver in eager, twitching expectation while waves of need pulsed between her thighs. She wanted to be strong.

"You've been a better wife to me in seven days than Lana was in ten full months," Kyros whispered. "More of a mother to Titus than any boy could ask. You're good for us. Both of us, and I don't want it to end. Ever. I want you to be my wife in truth."

She moved her head within his bracketing palms, trying to shake her head when all her body wanted to do was tell him yes.

"Marry me," he murmured against her lips before he claimed her mouth in yet another kiss. She groaned in involuntary surrender as his tongue delved deep, her will to protest eroded to mist. His talented lips, so, so convincing, teased and taunted hers, while she arched helplessly toward him.

His wide hands, now conversant in her curves, claimed her with shocking boldness, shaping her through the thick layers of soft cotton and flannel. She gasped as one hand closed over her breast at the same time that his other pulled her against the hard evidence of his desire. He kissed her, consuming her with erotic urgency while he ground the rigid length of his arousal against her. Her knees buckled, her thoughts scattered and she wilted against him even as she wrenched her mouth from beneath his.

"Wait—"

"No." He dragged her palm to his groin, pressing her hand against the long, hot ridge of his straining erection. "I want you to feel what you do to me. *You*. Not who you think you should be, but *you*."

"Kyros—"

He didn't let her finish her thought…any of her thoughts…

His kisses rained in insistent conviction over her averted face. His lips drifted over the curve of her eyebrow, the delicate flesh of her eyelid, the crest of her cheek and the sensitive slope of her neck. Even though her conscience rebelled, trying to reclaim her attention, she couldn't quite heed its call.

The powerful, demanding, thrilling details of Kyros waged a war she couldn't fight, imbuing her with a reckless sensuality she couldn't deny. But deny him she must. He wasn't for her. She knew it whether he did or not. If they were to marry, if she were to ignore her guilt and her apprehensions, it would infect the foundation of whatever they sought to build together. It would eventually erode both his respect for her and her respect for herself.

The thought of who she'd become once she'd lost herself to Kyros gave her resolve fresh strength. Desperate to escape, she wrenched free of his touch. Shaking, she backed away from him, her hands lifted between them. When he made a move as if to follow her, she stumbled back an additional step and gasped, "Don't."

Thankfully, he heeded her plea, though his eyes refused to release hers. For several protracted moments, no sounds except their strident breathing broke the silence. Finally, Laura mustered the courage to attempt speech. "You promised you wouldn't touch me."

"I have one more night with you as my wife."

"No." She paused, inhaling on a shaky thread of air. "I'm not your wife. I can't be. I can't even dress the part, remember? You need a wife who is like you are—someone who's comfortable in the world you inhabit, someone who can be your partner on the social scene, in your business dealings, and in your bed."

"I don't want that woman," he insisted. "I want you."

"You only think you do. I'm a challenge you haven't encountered before. But were I to relent, were I to agree to be your wife, I would change. The things you like the most

about me—the things I value most in myself—would disappear, and I'd resent you for it. I'd lose *me* to you, and I can't allow that to happen."

He stared at her with the firelight flickering across his granite profile, his eyes searching hers as if he were looking for a chink in her resolve. "Why are you so afraid of the woman you might become?"

She swallowed. Hitched her chin and braced her shoulders and refused to blink. "I'm not. I'm realistic. And you must not try to change my mind again. Promise me you won't, or I can't be Titus's nanny. I'll have to leave. Permanently."

His jade eyes glimmered with a hot flame of resistance. "I promise."

Dragging in a shuddering breath, she nodded. "Thank you."

"You'd better put space between us," he said grimly. "Because with you close enough to smell and touch, my promise isn't worth the breath it took me to say it."

She scuttled away to the far side of the room, staring at him with nervous eyes. "You aren't staying in here tonight, are you?" she asked.

"No." He bent to collect the half-empty bottle of ouzo and then strode to the closed door. "I find I have an appointment with the liquor cabinet that will last 'til morning."

And with that, he opened the door and left her, shivering and all alone with the big, white honeymoon bed they'd never shared.

CHAPTER FOURTEEN

For the next two weeks, Laura settled into the routine of caring for Titus in Kyros's spacious Athens home. She didn't see Kyros much at all, stealing only the occasional glimpse of him as he headed out to work or to yet another business meeting. She realized he was deliberately avoiding her, doing his best to honor his promise to her. He was allowing her to care for Titus without compromising her honor, and she was grateful for it.

At least that's what she told herself.

The fact that he was no longer trying to seduce her should have calmed her anxiety. But it didn't. Every time she caught sight of Kyros, of his drawn face and bloodshot eyes, her heart cramped with a longing so fierce she could scarcely breathe. The stress of being under the same roof as Kyros, trying to keep herself busy and not think about him, was proving to be a strain almost too difficult to bear.

Could she really do this long-term? Could she continue to live this way, even with Titus to buoy her spirits? She wasn't sleeping well, she wasn't eating well and she was in a constant state of agitated distraction.

Eager to get out of the house and away from the stress of imagining Kyros around every corner, she decided to take Titus to the park after a late lunch. The sky above was dark with angry clouds, and a mist of light rain gathered on

the surface of her brown overcoat and Titus's bright green snowsuit.

Shivering, but not dissuaded from her goal, she tightened her scarf. It was just a matter of time before the weather cleared. The sun would be out before they arrived at the park, and if it wasn't, she and Titus would just take a nice, relaxing drive in the rain.

What she hadn't factored into her plans, though, was the slickness of the wet, chilled roads. She'd barely made it halfway to the park before her brakes failed her and Kyros's car careened straight through an intersection.

A truck coming at her from the left slammed on its brakes and slid as well, spinning on its squealing tires until the sides of their vehicles collided in a bone-jarring thud. They spun together for several suspended seconds, staring wide-eyed and white-knuckled at each other until the truck's tires finally hit the curb and jolted them both to a shuddering stop.

Her first thought was of Titus, strapped into the backseat of the car and jarred into wakefulness by the impact. Panic shot through her limbs as she struggled to release her seat belt with clumsy, fumbling fingers, and clambered to the backseat to assess the damages. To her relief, Kyros's luxury car and his car seat had protected Titus from injury.

Even so, it took a good fifteen minutes for her shaking to subside. To think she'd been offended when Kyros questioned her ability to care for Titus. He'd been right. She'd involved her sweet, innocent nephew in a life-threatening car crash. All because she'd been too distracted by desire for Kyros to think properly.

Two hours later, after exchanging auto information, filing a police report and submitting to a barrage of medical tests, X-rays, and a volley of basic questions in the Athens's emergency room Laura secured Titus in his car seat and reached for her coat.

Aside from a welt on her shoulder from the seat belt and

a tender spot from where the airbag had scraped her fore-head, Laura had suffered no discernable injuries. But that didn't stop the nurses from trying to keep her at the hospital until Kyros arrived.

It didn't stop her from berating herself for being such a horrible, irresponsible person.

"I'm fine," she assured the trio of well-meaning nurses who'd crowded around her. "You heard the doctor. All our tests came out perfectly. Aside from this—" she gestured to the tender spot on her forehead "—you can't even tell we were involved in an accident."

"But Mr. Spyridis—"

"I wish you hadn't bothered him," Laura interrupted while a fresh pang of guilt cinched her stomach tight. "Really. We can just take a cab home."

Her departure was interrupted as Kyros flung the curtain to her room aside and roughly shouldered his way past the nurses to her side. "Laura!"

Startled to see him in such an obvious state of distress, Laura froze as he rushed forward to run his hands over her body, checking for injuries with frantic, probing fingers. With his shoulders covered in damp wool, his black hair glistening with fresh rain and his eyes snapping with green fire, he seemed like some avenging angel come to battle for her soul. Once he'd determined for himself that she'd suffered no permanent harm, he swore beneath his breath and hauled her up against his wet chest.

"What happened?" he asked against her hair.

"I was taking Titus to the park," she confessed, pressing back against his bracketing arms and staring hard at his chest. "I'm sorry," she whispered. "It was stupid of me. He could have been hurt. Or killed."

"It was an accident."

She flushed in denial, the clot of guilt moving up to her throat. "An accident that could have been avoided, had I been

thinking straight." She paused, gazing up at his eyes while her heart ached. "I wrecked your car."

"I don't give a damn about the car," he said thickly as he pulled her close again, his hand clamping hard over the back of her neck and his lips pressing against the top of her head.

Laura shivered within the folds of her coat, suddenly swamped with melancholy at the realization of how much she'd missed Kyros. She allowed him to hold her close, disturbed by the intensity of her emotions, by the poignant ache of pleasure of being touched by him—even if it was only to assess her for injuries—had wrought in her.

She didn't know why his mere presence, the gruff sound of his voice, could cause such a riot of emotions within her. But not knowing the reasons did not make their permanent separation any less necessary. After taking such a reckless risk with Titus just to escape her own thoughts, she couldn't stay in Athens any longer. Her judgment had been compromised, and she wouldn't be selfish enough to pretend otherwise. Remaining under Kyros's roof as Titus's nanny would benefit no one, Titus least of all.

Laura waited for the rain to stop, but near midnight, when the night sky still hadn't cleared, she realized she could no longer use the weather as an excuse to put off her departure. She'd already tucked Titus into bed for the final time and arranged for his previous nanny to return in the morning. She'd packed her bag with all the clothing that Kyros hated, changed the sheets in her bed and erased every last trace of her sojourn in Lana's life.

It was time.

Standing at Titus's crib, she stood watching him sleep while the ache of separation settled hard in her chest.

You can't stay. You know you can't.

She kissed her fingers and then pressed them gently

against Titus's soft curls, swallowing back the tears that filled her throat.

It took another five minutes for her to gather her courage and walk to Kyros's door. She stood for a long moment, staring at the unmoving span of white, before she lifted her knuckles to rap softly against the inset panel of wood.

Nothing.

She'd probably waited too long and Kyros was already asleep. That was good, wasn't it? Perhaps it would be better to leave without saying goodbye, and this was the universe's way of telling her to leave well enough alone. She'd knock one more time, softly, and if he didn't hear, she'd take it as her cue to go.

The door swung inward, leaving her closed fist suspended in midknock. Kyros stood there, rumpled and half-naked, his broad torso bare to the night air and a pair of black pajama pants slung low on his lean hips. His hair was a riot of tumbled curls and a shadow of a beard darkened the skin of his jaw and around his beautiful mouth.

Laura swallowed thickly, her throat dry and her heart clubbing against her ribs as he swiftly took in her traveling coat and the packed bag at her feet.

"Laura?" he said, his emerald gaze lifting to hers. "What's going on?"

"I've come to say goodbye," she told him.

His eyes widened at that. "Goodbye?"

"Yes."

"Why?"

She raised her chin, determined to remain businesslike, to keep all negotiations at bay. "Because I can't stay."

"Why not?"

"Because…" Her voice faltered. Quivered and died within the tight knot of her throat.

"You can't leave," he said.

"I—"

"No. I've kept my promise." His mouth pinched at the corners while his jaw clenched. "Aside from tonight, at the hospital, I haven't touched you. I haven't even talked to you. As hellish as it's been, I've left you alone so you could be with Titus."

She sucked in a steadying inhale. "I know," she admitted. "And I thought it would be enough, to have you out of sight." She forced herself to maintain eye contact. To appear strong. "But I was wrong."

His eyes narrowed. "I don't accept that."

She bit her lip, twisting her hands at her waist. "You have to. Knowing you're so close, even when I don't see you…it distracts me." Unable to continue looking at his face after such a damning confession, she dropped her gaze to the blue-and-white pattern of the carpet.

"I distract you?" he repeated in a rough voice.

She nodded miserably and told the floor. "When I see you, I can't think. When I don't see you, I'm a wreck. And Titus almost died today because of it."

"No." He reached for her chin, forcing her to look at him. "That was an accident," he said. "Titus is fine."

She stared at him through a sheen of tears. "This time, yes. But what about next time?"

"What next time? There doesn't have to be a next time."

She swallowed and averted her eyes despite his hold on her chin. "You're right. Because I'm leaving."

"No," he said gruffly, moving both hands to her face and dipping his knees until he met her eyes again. "Tell me what I have to do to make you stay. Whatever it is, just tell me, and I'll do it."

She closed her eyes, incapable of moving away from the sweet, forbidden touch of his fingers against her skin. "There's nothing you can do."

"There has to be."

She shook her head within his hands in abject misery. "I can't put Titus at risk. I won't."

"He needs you."

"He needs to be safe. And I can't be in your house without…" She pressed her lips together and struggled for composure while her throat thickened. She didn't move when he stepped forward to wrap his arms around her, or when his big hand rose to her nape and pulled her cheek against his bare chest. Her own hands lifted and clung, clutching at the wide expanse of his muscled back while she buried her face against the crisp black curls covering his heart. Desperate to touch him, she burrowed against him while sobs of regret, loneliness and want welled up within her chest.

"It doesn't have to be this way, you know," he muttered against her hair. "We can find another way."

"We can't."

"We can," he urged. "We can stop fighting what's between us and try to work with it instead."

Yes, a small voice agreed. *Stop fighting it. Just this once.* She could indulge in one night only, and then hold and cherish the memory of being with him when her future loomed ahead of her so bleak and empty. She could get drunk on him now, and deal with the guilt and the grief later.

The thought sent her pulse into a crazy, drumming rhythm while all the rational reasons for denying him were drowned out by her body's need. Fueled by the wild beating of her heart, she turned her head and lifted her mouth to his.

A muffled groan rumbled in his chest as he pulled her closer, lifting her to her toes. The shadowed hallway blurred and the salty tears stinging her nose were replaced with the musky scent of Kyros's skin. She reached to touch his rough jaw, his neck, the dark hair at his temples.

His fingers tightened against her ribs and the unyielding muscles of his chest pressed into her breasts. She clung to him, arching up and trying to get closer, closer, desperate

to assuage the aching sense of loss that threatened to overwhelm her.

Frantically, she withdrew enough to pluck at the stubborn buttons of her coat, yanking them free until she could shed the constricting layer of wool. Her fingers then moved to his black pajama pants, to the band of elastic that bisected the hard, warm plane of his abdomen. His hands lowered to hers, stilling her violent tugs.

"Laura…" he rasped. His nostrils flared while beneath her palm, she felt the leaping response of his body. His hands pulled her wrist back, creating a sliver of space between her fingers and his heat. "Once we do this, we can't undo it." He stared at her with glittering, dilated eyes. "I won't have your guilt on my conscience…you have to want it all, or we stop now."

Reckless now, she twisted free of his grasp and then reached to cup her hand over his hard, thickening length. He stiffened and she took advantage of his surprise to drag her open mouth over the black fleece covering his chest. When his hands rose to her upper arms, threatening to stall her efforts, she darted her tongue out to touch the tightly beaded tip of one brown nipple.

A grunt of pained pleasure vibrated beneath her hands and mouth. *"Theos,"* he gasped in a low, serrated voice.

She leaned forward into the warmth of his chest, rubbing her face and breasts against his bare skin. She tasted his flesh with wet, searching kisses until he claimed her, his arms banding tightly around her as his mouth dipped to cover hers.

He kissed her with ravenous, urgent strokes, guiding her into his dark bedroom and kicking the door behind her with a bare foot. Blackness descended, her senses suddenly heightening beneath the absence of sight.

She felt the hard planes of his body, the flexing of his ribs as he breathed in deep, unsteady draughts. She tasted the hint of mint and ouzo and sleep on his tongue, smelled the

musk and heat and salt of his skin, heard the thrumming of her pulse and the steady drum of rain hitting glass. Without breaking their kiss, she felt his hands at the front of her traveling dress, its dainty row of front buttons swiftly giving way to his nimble fingers. Her bra quickly followed suit, drifting to the floor in a flutter of silk and lace.

Time slowed to a crawl then, his mouth and fingers withdrawing to the barest hint of skimming touch as he painted electric whorls along her yearning flesh.

"Hurry," she begged him, leaning toward him as she tried to deepen the contact. "Kyros, please…" Now that she'd decided to steal this one night of passion with him, her earlier restraint had fled. She didn't care about right and wrong. She didn't care about regret or guilt. She wanted him *now*. She wanted his weight upon her, his long, thick heat deep, deep inside. She wanted his kisses, his skin, his breath. She wanted *him*.

"Hush," he murmured softly as he slowly dragged her slip down her trembling legs. She reached to touch him, but he stopped her, steering her backward until she felt the mattress against her thighs. He ran his hands up her arms, to the slope of her neck, and then he leaned to reach behind her.

A soft light clicked on, casting a glow over his gleaming shoulders and etching his features in gold.

"Kyros," she protested while a wave of self-consciousness claimed her. "What are you—?"

He silenced her with another kiss, his fingers climbing to release the pins from her hair. He nuzzled her lips as he dragged his fingers through the length of her hair, fanning it over her shoulders and chest. Leaning back with a crooked smile, he examined his handiwork. "I want to see you."

She raised an arm to cover the tips of her breasts, visible between dark strands of wavy hair. "Kyros—"

"All of you," he said as he pulled her arms to her sides. She flushed hotly, but remained still as his eyes darkened in their

perusal of her. After a few endless seconds, where modesty
and arousal warred, he boosted her up to sit on the edge of
the mattress. When she tried to scoot back, he stopped her
with a firm hold against her ankles. He planted her heels
against the bed frame and then stepped between her thighs.
"You don't know how I've dreamed of this."

Her reply was lost in a shuddering breath when he leaned
to kiss first one breast and then the other, the silky rasp of
his tongue teasing each straining tip to peaked awareness.

She tipped her chin to watch him as his broad back bowed
over her and his clever mouth tugged at her puckered nipples.
Just when she thought she could withstand no more, when
her fingers reached blindly for his shoulders to pull him up,
he sank lower, his big palms stroking the flesh of her thighs.

Sinking to his knees, he looked up at her before he leaned
to open a small drawer in his bedside table. She watched as
he rolled a condom over his jutting length, an eager, greedy
nervousness paralyzing her lungs. Sure that he'd come into
her now…now… She gasped when he pressed her knees apart
and then leaned to press a hot kiss against her inner thigh.
Her muscles drew tight and she tried to close her legs, feeling too vulnerable, too open. But he held her fast, and soon,
she was bucking toward him, clutching feverishly at his head
while he sucked and kissed at her aching entrance.

"Kyros," she gasped, her head arched back and every cell
in her body taut with need.

His tongue, hard and hot, dragged against that tight, swollen knot of desire, while his long, blunt fingers delved deep.
Stretching. Stroking. Massaging her virginal flesh into re-
silient pliancy. She felt her inner muscles clench, ripples of
pleasure rising to the crest. She hovered at the brink, spiraling higher, until he surged up to catch her mouth with his.
His hands shifted to her hips as he plundered her mouth, tipping her back while the plump head of his erection nudged
at her opening. The aching desire to have him deep inside

her was so sharp it hurt. She reached to guide his slippery length inside, thrilling at the way his thick, pulsing heat filled her palm.

"Laura," he said, his hands tightening against her while his breath fractured the air with shallow pants.

She hooked her calf around his buttocks and pulled, closing around his first hot inch. A stitch of pain knit her brow, but she forced herself to relax, to accept the stretching, sliding invasion.

"Theos." His arms trembled as they braced against her, his body suddenly still. "You're so small...."

"It's okay," she assured him, curling up to wrap her arms around him. She kissed his taut jaw and then tightened her legs around his thighs. "I want this." She pressed against him, sending him even deeper. "I want you."

He closed his eyes, his expression tight with desire. "I don't want to hurt you."

"I know." She did. She'd felt it in the way he'd touched her. And in the way he'd granted her space and time until she was ready to come to him. "I know."

He murmured something she couldn't understand and then sank low to kiss her. With his breathing ragged, his hands gripping hard against her hips, and his shoulder muscles rigid beneath her hands, he rocked incrementally deeper, each movement stretching, widening, filling.

She felt flushed and swollen and full. Everywhere. She felt the hard evidence of his desire, watched the intensity with which he lost himself in her, and a wellspring of love flooded her chest. Love she didn't want to feel. Love she didn't want to think about. So she pushed her thoughts aside. Later. She'd think about it later.

Tipping her hips toward him, she reached for his buttocks and pulled him deeper, watching as his nostrils flared. His breath hitched. The muscles in his neck stood out in ridges and his jaw bunched with knots, telling her how difficult

it was to retain control. She arched against him, her hands skimming up to the iron hardness of his shoulders as he seated himself deep against her womb.

He leaned to kiss her then, soft glancing kisses along her brow, the crests of her cheeks and her trembling lips. She stared into his intent green gaze as he began to move, watching her face the entire time. Slowly, incrementally, he withdrew, until only the barest hint of contact between them remained. She whimpered, trying to pull him back.

An equally slow slide brought him back.

Colors radiated on the edge of her vision and her hands moved to his hips as he slowly repeated the process again. And again. She gasped, marveling at the mounting pleasure, at the heated glide of flesh within flesh.

A low moan escaped her throat while her inner muscles quivered around him. The hard, aching peaks of her breasts begged for relief, for his mouth, his hands, anything. Anything to assuage the building tension. And still he continued his slow, sensual assault.

His thumb dipped low between their bodies to flick against the tight nub of nerves hidden deep within her folds. Inside her mouth, his tongue mimicked the motions below. And then his finger slid down to circle the tight rim of flesh surrounding his rigid length.

She jerked in response, her entire body feeling flushed and hot and wild. "Kyros…"

"Tell me what you want."

"I want…" She closed her eyes and reached for his arms, clinging to him as his movements grew faster, more insistent, pushing her toward the edge while incoherent murmurings tumbled from her lips.

"That's right. Tell me. Tell me what you want to feel."

So she did, urging him to push harder, faster, to touch and lick and suck until the tightness within blossomed into shards of light. Light filled her heart, her lungs and womb until she

saw only white. She felt drowned in sensation and heard the rushing of her own pulse within her ears. While her body's pleasure rippled hard around his length, he gripped her face and told her she was beautiful and *his* and how he'd never let her go. And when she started to drift down, he stroked deep within her, branding her, making her pleasure peak yet again as his name tore from her throat. He answered her cry with one of his own, grunting out his triumphant release as he drove into her one last time and exploded, his muscles tightening to stone.

Afterward, feeling lush and pliant and utterly relaxed, Laura leaned her forehead against his chest and inhaled the scent of their lovemaking. Slight tremors still pulsed at the place where they joined, and the realization of the intimacy they'd shared made a blend of joy and anguish collect in her throat.

She'd never realized lovemaking could be so beautiful.

She'd never realized that leaving could hurt so much.

CHAPTER FIFTEEN

KYROS HAD spent his life chasing the things he wanted, and he'd never once failed in catching whatever he'd set his sights upon. Quitting was not part of his vocabulary. He'd had his share of setbacks, but he'd never lost sight of his goals. He'd always known that with time and effort and sheer persistence, he would prevail.

But waking up alone and then discovering Laura had left despite their lovemaking was the first time he'd doubted his ability to succeed. He felt defeated. Vanquished. Maybe even a little bit crazed.

Realizing that what he offered wasn't enough for her, that she still, *still* hid from him made him feel viciously, bitterly inadequate in a way he'd never felt before. It made him want to beat his fists against the cold, unyielding walls that surrounded his home.

Theos. What a fool he'd been. He should have realized the truth the moment he'd concocted his flawed plan to bring her home. She'd been right about him, right about the lies he'd told. He'd used his grandmother and his son to manipulate her. He'd blackmailed her into staying with him, and now, he was paying the price for his sins.

Laura needed someone whom she could love without guilt, a man who was as kind and selfless as she. Compared to her, Kyros was willful, ruthless, harsh and unforgiving. He was

a bully and everyone knew it. No wonder she felt the need to protect herself from him. No wonder she hid her vulnerable, sweet and fragile heart from him. She didn't trust him. And why would she?

So no matter how his soul howled at him to snatch her back, he wouldn't bully Laura into staying. He wouldn't chase her down and force her to return. He owed her that much. If she didn't return of her own volition, if she didn't trust him enough to choose him, he would allow her to go.

But he'd be damned if he'd be happy about it.

Scowling, Kyros withdrew to his study for a much-needed drink.

"What!" he snarled forty-eight miserable hours later when he yanked open his door to find his tense butler standing next to his grandmother and her nurse.

"Is this a bad time?" *Giagiá's* said wryly.

"Giagiá," he said. "What are you doing here?"

"I have decided to accept your offer to live with you here." She eyed his unshaven face, rumpled hair and obvious state of steady intoxication. "Though I can see I should have called first to discover if I am still welcome."

Guilt and anger and a fear he refused to acknowledge vied for dominance as he looked down at his grandmother. "Of course you're still welcome."

"After spending the holidays with you, I realized I was being stubborn for no good reason. Having time with family is more important than a pile of marble and stone."

"I'm glad to hear you've come to your senses."

"Yes. Except I—"

"I'll have two rooms prepared for you right away."

"No, Kyros. I was wrong to come. Seeing you now, it is obvious that my moving here will be an imposition and—"

"No. Stay. I insist." He motioned for silence as he instructed Admes to accompany his grandmother's nurse to a guest suite and to have their things collected.

When he returned his gaze to *Giagiá,* it was to find her brow pleated with worry. "Perhaps you should check with Lana first."

Guilt stabbed his gut. "I don't need to check with Lana. You'll stay."

She studied his taut features for a moment before she said, "Your wife deserves a say in who shares her home."

"Lana's gone," he finally admitted in a tight voice. "Permanently."

"What? Why?"

Theos. Why the hell had he thought lying to her would be a good idea?

"Kyros," *Giagiá* scolded, her worry sharpening her voice. "Why is Lana gone?"

Rather than answer, he wheeled her into his study, settled into his black couch and then reached for her frail hands. Fear clamped his chest with a vicelike fist as he searched for the words he'd never planned to say. "There's something I chose not to tell you because I was worried it would upset you," he said as he stared into her concerned eyes. "Something that I should have told you a long time ago."

She stiffened as if preparing for a blow, her expression guarded as her gaze searched his. "What is it?"

He found his throat too tight to form words.

"Kyros?"

"Lana is not returning because…" He forced himself not to look away. "Because she died."

"What?" she asked as the color leeched from her lined face.

He simply stared at her, waiting for his words to sink in while he fought the guilt that roiled deep in his belly.

"How?" Her mouth moved wordlessly for a few seconds before she asked, "When?"

He felt his jaw flex and his gut tightened with dread.

"And why did you not tell me?" she asked.

"I didn't tell you…" He swallowed a curse, damning his weakness while he tightened his grip around her hands. "Because I was a coward."

"And because I am dying," she said, twisting her hands free of his. "You thought I was too weak to handle the truth."

"I didn't want to disappoint you," he clarified, determined not to lie any longer. "I wanted you to believe I was the man you raised me to be."

She stared at him, visibly confused. "I do not understand."

"I only married Lana because I got her pregnant. And then she left me. Months ago."

"What?"

"And when she died, I didn't even grieve. I was glad."

Giagiá's features puckered with confusion. "But that cannot be true. I know how much you love her. I saw the way—"

"No. You didn't. That woman was Lana's twin sister, Laura."

"Her twin—? But why would she…why would *you*—?"

"Because I wanted to give you the holiday you deserved to have." His chest tightened, making it hard to continue his confession. But he plowed forward anyway. "I didn't want to admit what a fool I'd been with her sister."

"I am sure—"

"I couldn't stomach the thought of you seeing how much like my father I'd become."

She studied him with her soft green eyes and then slowly shook her head. "You are nothing like that wretched man, Kyros," *Giagiá* told him. "Nothing."

His jaw tightened, self-disgust roiling through his gut. "No? I blackmailed a kind, beautiful and innocent woman into posing as Lana," he said, the back of his neck growing hot with shame. "I *lied* to you."

Giagiá cocked her head, her perceptive gaze tracking the signs of fatigue around his mouth and eyes. "Yes, you did. But you lied because you wanted me to be happy."

"It doesn't make it right."

"No, it does not," she said, after a moment. "But it makes it understandable. And the outcome was as you wished. I had a lovely holiday. The happiest I have had since your grandfather died."

He shook his head, rejecting her easy forgiveness. "It was a lie."

"So make it truth," she said, as if the solution to everything were well within his reach. "Fix it."

Her words felt like an invisible punch to the gut. "I can't. I tried." The truth of it had crouched in his gut for far too long for him to dismiss it. "She doesn't want me."

"Nonsense. I saw the way she lit up whenever you came into the room."

Theos. If losing Laura hadn't killed him, this discussion surely would. "She deserves someone better."

"Oh, Kyros," she chided softly. "Why must you always doubt yourself? Why can you not believe that you are a good man, worthy of love?"

"Because I'm not," he murmured while the knotted ache in his gut developed yet another layer.

"Of course you are." She lifted a weathered hand to his cheek and offered him a small, sad smile. "You always have been."

The back of his throat started to burn and his eyes blurred, stinging while he tried to blink the uncomfortable emotion away.

"Go fetch your wife, Kyros."

"She's not my wife," he said, his voice low enough that it wouldn't betray how close he was to breaking down.

"She is the wife of your heart, whether you are legally married or not. And she is Titus's mother. Any fool can see it."

He nodded in miserable agreement, struggling to curb the tide of emotions threatening to unman him. He'd brought this

on himself. He'd forced Laura to lie, to play his wife and a mother to his son. But he'd not stopped to consider the consequences. He'd not stopped to consider that he would fall in love with her.

"Go."

"No." He swallowed and lifted his eyes. "I forced her hand once before. I won't do it again," he vowed raspily. "If she comes back, it will be because she wants to."

Three interminable months later, after yet another despondent night of no sleep and restless longing for what could never be, Laura lay in her solitary bed staring listlessly at the ceiling while the weak light of dawn crept into its corners. It was the same ceiling she'd stared at her entire life. The same crack, blamed on the house's settling decades ago, stretched its gnarled finger toward the window casing. The gingham curtains, their pattern faded to that of old newsprint, revealed the narrow alley behind the house.

"This is what I want," she said aloud, discouraged by her inability to recapture her previous contentment. "I want this life."

Didn't she? She'd spent all her adult years, and most of her adolescent years as well, becoming the person she was meant to be. The life she'd planned on, worked toward and expected to enjoy was here, well within her reach. And yet… and yet, the happiness she'd thought to feel remained frustratingly, achingly, out of reach.

Returning to her life in Oregon and embracing the routines that had brought her such comfort in the past no longer felt right. Her few short weeks with Kyros and Titus had changed her.

She was *different*. She'd gotten drunk on ouzo, she'd mothered an infant boy and she'd fallen prey to passion. She'd made love, felt alive and whole for the first time in her life,

and the experience had fueled her with a burning, restless longing for more.

But wanting more was Lana's domain. It had never, ever been hers. Laura had prided herself on being happy with her lot in life, with making the most of her limited resources and finding contentment with the small things.

Wanting more made her weak. Desperate. Vulnerable. She refused to be the woman who went hot with desire simply because a man looked at her with smoldering green eyes. She refused to be the woman who wanted things she couldn't have. She closed her eyes and rolled to her side, wrapping her arms around her middle and trying to deny the truth that pushed and pushed and pushed at her consciousness.

She refused to want the life Lana had thrown away.

Breathing hard, her chest tight and her throat working in disconcerting spasms, she fought the wave of longing that swamped her lungs. Her eyes stung and the back of her nose burned while tremors of truth burrowed their way to the surface.

Gulping back the tide of tears she could no longer contain, she wept into the silence of her small, shadowed room. Her shuddering whimpers evolved into sobs and soon, her face and pillow and hands were wet.

Oh, God. She did want the life Lana had thrown away. She wanted love and Kyros and Titus. She wanted it more than she wanted her next breath. And she'd turned her back on it all because she'd been afraid to reach for a happiness she couldn't control.

She'd left because she'd been terrified of opening herself up to the pain of rejection and loss. That had been her real reason for refusing Kyros. It had nothing to do with the fact that he'd been married to Lana. It had to do with her own inability to allow herself to feel or to trust anyone to get close. If her own twin hadn't loved her and had found pleasure in hurting her, how could she trust Kyros to feel any differently?

It had always been so much easier to hold herself apart, to be the spectator who attended to others' needs and ignored her own. She didn't know how to rely on anyone but herself. She didn't know how to offer her happiness up to another's hands. And yet what choice did she have? She was miserable.

Suddenly, a desperate urge to return to Kyros *now* had her flinging back the covers and stumbling toward her closet. She wanted to drive to the airport and take the first plane to Greece. She wanted to throw herself on his mercy and beg him to take her back, to forgive her for making such a colossal mess of things.

She wanted to beg him to let her try again. To convince her that she could be brave.

CHAPTER SIXTEEN

By the time Laura arrived on Kyros's doorstep thirty-six hours later, she was a nervous wreck. Even with her stomach in knots, her body wrapped in a sapphire silk that made her blush and her breathing a shallow imitation of what it should be, Kyros's big, asymmetrical mansion in the waning light of evening still brought a poignant rush of homecoming. She entered the gate's code with numb fingers, wondering how everyone would react to her unannounced arrival. Trepidation mounted as she stopped, frozen before the tall, dark door.

Before she could muster the courage to knock, the door swung soundlessly open to reveal the butler's impassive visage. Only a faint widening of his dark eyes betrayed his surprise as he bowed and then straightened before ushering her over the threshold. "Ms. Talbot."

"I'm sorry for not calling ahead," she blurted in jittery explanation. "I meant to, of course, but then I couldn't get service in the airports and my phone's battery died and I forgot my charger and I—"

"Admes, who is it?"

Laura recognized Iona's voice before she saw Kyros's grandmother. The old woman's frail body looked even smaller, more bowed, as she wheeled her chair toward the entryway.

"Laura?" the old woman breathed as her chair drew to a stop. "Is it really you?"

Laura blinked as a fresh onslaught of emotion swept through her. "Iona?"

Iona reached for Laura's cold hands and squeezed them between her own. "You have come."

"Yes, but I—"

"Hush. It does not matter. It only matters that you are here."

She swallowed, unsure of how to interpret Iona's words. "Is he in?"

"Yes," Iona said, her wizened face managing to look both hopeful and worried at the same time. "He spends his evenings in his office now," she said. "Upstairs. Where I cannot see his upset or scold him for drinking."

Laura inhaled sharply at that, and then nodded.

"Do you plan to stay?"

"If he'll have me," she answered on a faint whisper.

Relief seemed to grant Iona fresh color and strength. "If anyone can convince him, it is you."

Before she had time to press for details, Iona and Admes made their excuses and disappeared from view. Realizing that she would have to face Kyros on her own, should she be brave enough to do so, sent Laura's pulse into a wild rhythm against her eardrums.

At the top of the grand staircase, her hand slick against the banister, she turned left and walked toward his office. The windows at the west end glowed with sunset's glorious palette, and her feet slowed as she reached the corner. Her gaze darted from the closed door of Kyros's office, to the darkening horizon outside, to her own trembling hands.

Shivering, she wished she'd worn something less risky than the formfitting sapphire bridesmaid dress she'd chosen. But safety didn't make her happy. So she gathered her cour-

age, her resolve, and all her hopes and dreams for a future with the man she wanted and loved.

The silver handle turned without a sound and she pushed the door open to reveal a room as dark as dusk. No lights were on and long shadows stretched from the hulking furniture, across the carpeted floor and into the darkened corners of the room.

Kyros's office smelled faintly of him, a subtle blend of musk, winter breezes and man. The bare windows, stretching from floor to ceiling on two entire walls, offered an unobstructed view of the grounds, the city lights and the distant sea. During the day, with the sun streaming in and his property stretched out below, the room would be awash with light and color. Now, though, the shadows and encroaching darkness only magnified her trepidation.

A glinting movement caught her eye and she found Kyros's tall silhouette at the center of the farthest dark window. A tumbler of liquid swirled in his large, square hand as he stared outside, the rest of his body tense and still. Laura froze, her gaze taking in his wide back and broad shoulders, his tapered waist and powerful thighs. She'd forgotten how big he was, forgotten how just looking at him could send a shiver of longing through her limbs.

He'd dressed in dark pants and a white shirt, and the rolled shirtsleeves, a pale gray in the waning light, contrasted sharply with his tanned forearms. Even from the back, he looked imposing. Hard. His black hair was rumpled and in need of a trim, and as she watched, he took a punishing swallow of his drink and then the tumbler clinked against the window as he pressed his fist against the glass.

Her stomach seized as he lifted his other fist to the window and then slumped between his upraised arms, his head sinking low between his bowed shoulders. It was the most dejected she'd ever seen him, and she ached to gather him close, to kiss him and hold him and beg him to forgive her.

She swallowed, her throat clenching in trepidation, before she finally managed to whisper a weak "Kyros?"

His body stiffened and his head lifted by incremental degrees, the muscles in his back bunching as he slowly turned to see her.

Her mouth went dry as she surveyed his haggard face, the evidence of too many nights spent drinking stamped across his ashen features. His glittering green eyes, almost black in the waning light, seemed to have lost their spark. Gone was the teasing, flirtatious glint of humor. In its stead was only flat indifference that told her she should have stayed home.

"What are you doing here?"

"I…I had to see you."

"Why?"

Her entire soul quailed at his pending rejection, but she'd come too far to turn coward now. "Because I…I realized I was wrong…about me…about everything."

A tense silence spun out between them, its fingers of doubt and fear wrapping tightly around her throat and lungs.

"No," he finally said. "You were right."

"But I wasn't!" she blurted, her heart clamping in hard, swift denial. "I was a fool to cling to things that don't matter, to fight what we had…. I was wrong and scared and afraid…but I don't want to fight it anymore. I don't want to pretend that I'm—"

"Laura, stop." Kyros's low voice cut off her protest. "We both know why you left, and it wasn't a mistake. Being with me *will* change you." A brittle frown tugged at one corner of his mouth. "And not for the better, I'm afraid."

"No, Kyros—"

"I'll admit I was so blinded by lust for a few weeks that I forgot all the reasons things could never work between us. But I've discovered that with time and enough ouzo, I can accept the truth. I can accept that you deserve a better man and that you did what needed to be done." He lifted his half-

empty tumbler, his eyes a scorching flame of green. "I can't blame you for being strong when I was too weak to send you away myself."

"No," she insisted shakily. "Wait. You don't understand. I wasn't strong. I was a coward. I was running away and I—"

"Laura—"

"No," she interrupted. "Let me finish. After I've said what I've come to say, you can tell me I'm wrong. But hear me out before you decide. Please."

He stared at her in silence for several long, nerve-racking seconds before he moved to his desk and sank into the big, dark chair behind it. "Fine." His tumbler clinked on the flat, polished surface and then he reached to refill his glass with another hefty splash of liquor. "Talk."

While she watched him, uncertain of how to begin now that he'd granted her the time to plead her case, he leaned back in his chair and downed another deep swallow of the ouzo, his eyes remaining fixed on hers.

Laura inhaled, balled her fists at her thighs and plunged headlong into confession she'd been too terrified to even think about forty-eight hours ago. "I love you," she said in a rush. "I never wanted to feel this way about you, but I do." As difficult as it was, she wouldn't allow herself to drop her gaze. She'd lay her soul bare and make herself vulnerable to him, no matter the cost. "If I could have, I'd have buried myself in Oregon and never looked back. But I can't. As much as I tried, I can't. I've changed and I can't be the person I used to be. I've lived my entire life hiding from my own wants and needs, and I can't do that anymore. I need you."

She blinked, the truth of her claim settling deeper into her bones. "You can imagine how difficult this is for me to admit aloud, because I've turned self-denial into an art form. I've actually taken pride in how selfless I'd learned to be. It took you, calling my bluff, to realize what a fool I've been."

He didn't respond, other than staring at her while his hand

slowly, slowly spun the tumbler of ouzo upon the surface of the desk.

"I can't blame it on Lana, either," she continued raggedly. "Because the truth is, it wasn't Lana who pushed me into my rigid, self-righteous shell. It was me. I learned early on that if I didn't want anything, I couldn't be disappointed. No one could take it away or hurt me by withholding it if I didn't want it. So I've never allowed myself to need anyone. Ever. As long as I kept myself separate, as long as I didn't let anyone see the desperate, lonely person inside, I couldn't be hurt. I'd be invincible and strong."

She pressed a fist against her belly, against the persistent ache that never seemed to wane. "But I was wrong. Rather than fight for what I wanted, for what I *needed,* I hid. I told myself I was being good. That I was being selfless. That I was caring for others and putting their needs first. But it was all a lie. I was just protecting myself. Avoiding risk and lying to those who could have made me happy."

She searched Kyros's dark face for a clue to his reaction, but he remained utterly still.

"When I fell in love with you, my shell cracked," she continued in a frayed voice, "I couldn't keep the pieces together anymore. You made me *feel* when I'd never allowed myself to feel before. And it frightened me. I didn't know how to handle being vulnerable. I didn't know how to *want* without being terrified of the loss that would surely come because of it. So I used Lana as a wedge between us. I used your marriage to her as an excuse to shore up my own crumbling defenses."

She paused, her heart in her throat, as she surveyed Kyros's inscrutable features. His expression hadn't changed at all, but a flush of color had darkened the crests of his cheeks and his fingertips had turned white where they gripped the glass of liquor.

"And then I had the accident with Titus, and it gave me the perfect excuse to escape. But when I tried to…to say

goodbye and we…" She closed her eyes, too overwrought to maintain the illusion of strength. "I never knew it could be like that," she confessed through a tight throat. "Being with you…I lost myself. I lost everything. And it terrified me. I'd never lost control before. Ever. I tried to regain it by returning to my old life, to the things that used to matter. But it didn't work. I know what it's like to love someone now, and I can't erase that knowledge. I can't." Her voice cracked. "Please, Kyros. I know I don't deserve you and I know it's too late, but if there's any way that I can convince you to give me another chance, to let me love you, I swear I will never hide from you again."

He still hadn't moved, still hadn't said a word, and his cold, impenetrable silence settled over her like a funereal shroud. She was too late, she could feel it, and the realization made her entire body ache with a loss she didn't know how to absorb.

A sharp, clawing pain burned in her chest and spread outward, leaving a cold, leaden lump of fear in its wake. What would she do, now that she'd lost him? Where would she go? What would she do? How could she return to a life that held no joy, no love and no hope? Staring hard at her white, white hands, she swallowed convulsively and prayed she could keep herself together long enough to escape before breaking down.

Her vision blurred and her breath hitched, and she realized with a humiliating rush that she wouldn't be able to keep her tears at bay. She was going to humiliate herself even more, and the pain and embarrassment of it had her stumbling back, her hand clamped hard over her mouth. The thought of breaking into sobs while he watched her so dispassionately was more than she could bear. With a wretched cry, she spun away from his desk and lurched toward the door.

He caught her before she could escape, his big hands pulling her back. A tortured sound escaped her throat and then he was spinning her, and glaring down at her distressed face.

Too unmoored to determine his intent, Laura's body bowed in an effort to break free. His grip only tightened, lifting her to her toes, and then, to her utter astonishment, he hauled her forward and crushed her against his chest.

"Damn you," he cursed before dipping his cheek against hers and banding his arms around her back. "Do you know the hell you've put me through these past three months?"

"I'm sorry," she sobbed while her lungs quaked in relief. "So, so sorry. I've been such a coward and I was so afraid—"

"*Theos,* Laura. Don't you know you never have to be afraid of me?" he interrupted, pushing her back until he could search her face with his green, green gaze. "Don't you know I'd give my life before I hurt you?"

She nodded through a blur of tears, her heart contracting with painful joy. "I wanted to believe it. I did. And I hoped…"

"I love you, Laura. I've loved you from the first minute I saw you." His hands lifted to the sides of her face, bracketing her head between his palms. "Believing I'd lost you almost killed me."

"I'm sorry," she whispered.

"Promise me you'll never put me through that again," he ordered gruffly.

"I promise."

"Promise me you'll marry me, and never leave me again."

"Yes," she breathed, reaching to pull his mouth to hers. "I promise."

He obliged her silent plea, ravaging her mouth with brutal, pent-up passion. A flood of heat swept over Laura, and she returned his kiss with all the love and yearning she'd denied while they were apart. When he withdrew enough for her to catch her breath, he muttered, "Come to my bed."

She nodded and then he lifted her into his arms, swinging her up as he carried her out of his office, down the hall and into his room. She gasped when he tossed her upon the bed and then fell upon her. She had no time to protest before

he'd stripped her of her coat, her blue dress, her underwear and bra. He divested himself of his own clothing with the same degree of urgency, yanking hard at buttons and zippers and shoes, ripping seams when they failed to cooperate quickly enough. She reached to help him, tugging at cotton and wool until he leaned over her, naked and glorious and ready to plunder.

And oh, how she wanted him to plunder her. Fast, slow, hard, soft, she didn't care. She wanted it all. Now.

Knowing that his powerful body, every long and lean and sculpted inch of it, was hers for the taking sent a hot quiver of yearning through her. She inhaled sharply, savoring the anticipation even as she wanted it to end. "Oh, Kyros, I've missed you so much." She leaned up to press herself against all that hot, burnished flesh, burrowing against his hard chest and wrapping her arms as far as they would extend around his broad back.

A rumble of agreement sounded from deep within his chest and then he was rolling her to the side, his warm body taut alongside hers and his big arms wrapped around her. He rocked her for a moment, flesh against flesh, and then she felt his hand lift to her disheveled hair. "Do you know how hard it was for me to wait for you to return?" He breathed against her cheek. When she didn't answer, he tipped her face back and rubbed a thumb over her temple, searching her eyes as if he sought to memorize the person she'd hidden within. "When you left, I felt like half of me was gone. I was crazed. Desperate. Every day, I drove halfway to the airport before I forced myself to turn back."

"Why did you?"

His thumb stilled while his voice turned to gravel. "Because I needed it to be your decision. I needed to know that the choice to be with me was yours."

"It was. From the very beginning, it was. I told myself it

was all for Titus, but I think, even then, that I wanted to be near you."

He smiled, his eyes warm. "Not as much as I wanted to be with you."

"But you thought I was Lana."

"No. My body—my heart—it knew the truth the first moment I saw you." He turned his hand, grazing her skin with his knuckle. The soft stroke moved from her cheek to her neck, to the valley between her breasts and down to the curve of her belly. "One look, and I knew I had to have you." He leaned to press his lips against the center of her chest, lingering for just a moment while her heart beat against his mouth.

"So you decided to make me yours," she added faintly. "Even if you had to blackmail me to do it."

"Yes. I wanted you too much to allow you to leave. I was unscrupulous in my efforts, I'll admit, but in the end, it was worth it."

"Yes. It was," she agreed, her heart so full she could scarcely contain it.

"I love you, Laura Talbot," he said softly. "More than I ever thought possible."

"I love you, too."

"Prove it," he said in a low voice. Her pulse quickened as she felt his knee wedge its way between her thighs while the hot, silken insistence of his sex nudged her abdomen. "Prove you love me and that you'll never leave me again."

"Show me how, and I will," she promised, reaching to kiss his mouth. "Show me, and I'll do it. Whatever you want."

Banked passion flared to life in his emerald eyes. "Whatever I want?"

"Yes," she whispered.

"It's been three months without any relief," he warned. "My appetites may shock you."

A small thrill went through her at his words. "Then shock me," she dared him, tiny sparks of sensation gathering at

every place they touched. "Show me how to make it up to—"
A gasp cut her short as Kyros bent to claim her nipple. It contracted sharply, beading into a hard, throbbing point as he teased it with his teeth and tongue. She tensed, arched and pressed against him as pleasure streaked along her nerve endings. A moan collected in her throat and she lifted beneath him, pulling him closer with her arms as he drew the peak of her breast deep, deep into his mouth.

She began to shift restlessly against him, pressing down against the long, hair-dusted surface of his thigh as he sucked and kissed and bit. "Please…" she begged. "I need you."

"I know," he murmured as his fingers slid incrementally lower. He teased her, circling and feinting within her curls, his soft, glancing strokes spreading moisture and heat and a sharp, aching desire for more. Gasping, she reached for his hand and dragged it lower, bucking beneath him as one long finger finally slid home.

She moaned, insensate, as his mouth covered hers in a scorching kiss and his palm exerted a steady, rocking pressure against her. His weight shifted and she reached blindly for the heavy, heated silk of his sex. Curling her fingers around the thick shaft, she guided him toward the apex of her thighs, arching toward him and nudging him closer with her feet and legs and hips.

"Not yet, *mikri mou,*" he breathed against her mouth, his voice a rough rasp of restraint. "We have all night."

"But I want you now." She surged up against him, raining desperate kisses against his chest and neck and jaw. "Please. I don't want to wait. I want you…I need you. Now."

"Now?" he repeated in a hoarse murmur.

"Yes." She felt like she couldn't get close enough, as if all the loneliness and separateness of her entire life had distilled down to this one moment. She needed him to dispel the fear, to eradicate the wanting and all her unmet needs.

Taut and trembling, she squeezed her eyes shut and begged, "Love me, Kyros. Please love me now."

"All right," he breathed. Shifting to his knees, he eased her knotted hands from his back and lifted her arms above her head. "But only if you open your eyes."

When she complied, he leaned to press a gentle kiss against her mouth. "I love you," he said as he slowly lowered his sleek body into the cradle of her hips. "Always," he promised, nudging his sex against her hot, swollen crease.

The broad tip slipped just barely inside, and pleasure seized her within its scorching, clamping grip.

"Stay with me," he said, leaning on his elbows as he cradled her face between his palms when her eyes drifted closed again. "Don't hide from this."

Dragging her eyes open, she forced herself to meet his gleaming gaze. It didn't seem possible that she could open to him any more than she already had, or that the poignant intimacy between them could increase. But it did. Amazingly, it did. She felt tears gather at the back of her throat, felt the sting of emotion prick at her eyes, and then gasped aloud as he slid deeper.

"I love you," he repeated as he pressed inside her, a sleek, penetrating invasion that touched both her heart and her womb. He rocked, spreading her thighs with his own, until she could no longer discern where she ended and he began. "Do you believe me?"

She nodded wordlessly while tears seeped into her hair, her neck and torso arching involuntarily as he nudged forward and then back again. He slowly increased the length and speed of his strokes, until his own muscles grew taut with strain and a fine mist of sweat beaded on his brow. And still he watched her, his chest brushing the tight, reddened tips of her breasts while his movements below kindled a driving, rising pulse of pleasure.

"Tell me," he urged, his rhythm driving her further toward the peak. "Tell me you're mine. Always."

"Forever," she cried, the feel of him so wrenching, so… unimaginably good, she no longer had control of her own voice. The confession tumbled from her mouth, urging him forward with vows of love and hope and commitment. "I love you, Kyros…always… I can't live without you…. I need you…."

He thrust hard then, shoving her several inches up the bed while his hands gripped hers and his eyes bored into hers. She shattered and convulsed, her body and emotions clenching in concert while intense joy overwhelmed her, rippling from her womb to the outer reaches of her skin. Watching her, he suddenly tightened above her, his body arching into a tight, steely bow of pumping muscle and gleaming skin while her name ripped from his throat.

"Can I close my eyes now?" she asked a few minutes later, after he'd collapsed atop her and pressed a warm kiss to the side of her damp neck.

A low rumble of laughter accompanied the question and he rolled to the side, taking her with him. Still joined, a warm glow radiating from head to toe, she felt a sense of lightness—of rightness—she'd never dared to want before.

"Thank you for returning to me," he whispered as he reached to tuck a strand of loose hair behind her ear.

Feeling bashful now, she flushed. "I had no choice. You're the only one who can show me who I am really am."

"There are a lot of things I plan to show you," he told her with a soft, teasing smile. He ran a finger along her cheek and down to the tip of her chin. "I want to spend the rest of my life helping you discover who you are," he said, "and learning who we can become. Together."

"Oh, Kyros," she said wonderingly, raising her fingers to his dear face. "What did I ever do to deserve you?"

He shifted his hips just a bit, nudging his hardening length

inside her yet again. "You only needed to be yourself, *agápi mou*."

Her eyes widened at his unexpected thickness. "Really?" she gasped breathlessly.

"Really," he agreed with a wicked grin, before he convinced her all over again.

* * * * *

COMING NEXT MONTH from Harlequin Presents®
AVAILABLE JULY 31, 2012

#3077 THE SECRETS SHE CARRIED
Lynne Graham
Erin and Christophe's passionate affair ended harshly.
Years later, he's bent on revenge, until Erin drops two very
important bombshells!

#3078 THE MAN BEHIND THE SCARS
The Santina Crown
Caitlin Crews
Rafe McFarland—Earl of Pembroke and twenty-first-century
pinup—has secretly wed tabloid darling Angel in the newest
Santina scandal!

#3079 HIS REPUTATION PRECEDES HIM
The Lyonedes Legacy
Carole Mortimer
Eva is hired to decorate Markos Lyonedes's apartment, but
the notorious playboy makes it difficult for her to stay out of
the bedroom!

#3080 DESERVING OF HIS DIAMONDS?
The Outrageous Sisters
Melanie Milburne
Billionaire Emilio Andreoni needs one thing: the perfect
woman. That was once Gisele Carter until headline-grabbing
scandals made her the not-so-perfect fiancée!

#3081 THE MAN SHE SHOULDN'T CRAVE
Lucy Ellis
Dating agency owner Rose is in over her head with a new PR
proposal involving ruthless Russian ice-hockey team owner
Plato Kuragin!

#3082 PLAYING THE GREEK'S GAME
Sharon Kendrick
Few dare to defy global hotel magnate Zac Constantinides—
but he's met his match in feisty designer Emma!

REQUEST YOUR FREE BOOKS!

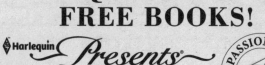

2 FREE NOVELS PLUS
2 FREE GIFTS!

YES! Please send me 2 FREE Harlequin Presents® novels and my 2 FREE gifts (gifts are worth about $10). After receiving them, if I don't wish to receive any more books, I can return the shipping statement marked "cancel." If I don't cancel, I will receive 6 brand-new novels every month and be billed just $4.30 per book in the U.S. or $4.99 per book in Canada. That's a saving of at least 14% off the cover price! It's quite a bargain! Shipping and handling is just 50¢ per book in the U.S. and 75¢ per book in Canada.* I understand that accepting the 2 free books and gifts places me under no obligation to buy anything. I can always return a shipment and cancel at any time. Even if I never buy another book, the two free books and gifts are mine to keep forever.

106/306 HDN FERQ

Name	(PLEASE PRINT)
Address	Apt. #
City	State/Prov.	Zip/Postal Code
Signature (if under 18, a parent or guardian must sign)	

Mail to the **Reader Service:**
IN U.S.A.: P.O. Box 1867, Buffalo, NY 14240-1867
IN CANADA: P.O. Box 609, Fort Erie, Ontario L2A 5X3

Not valid for current subscribers to Harlequin Presents books.

**Are you a current subscriber to Harlequin Presents books and want to receive the larger-print edition?
Call 1-800-873-8635 or visit www.ReaderService.com.**

* Terms and prices subject to change without notice. Prices do not include applicable taxes. Sales tax applicable in N.Y. Canadian residents will be charged applicable taxes. Offer not valid in Quebec. This offer is limited to one order per household. All orders subject to credit approval. Credit or debit balances in a customer's account(s) may be offset by any other outstanding balance owed by or to the customer. Please allow 4 to 6 weeks for delivery. Offer available while quantities last.

Your Privacy—The Reader Service is committed to protecting your privacy. Our Privacy Policy is available online at www.ReaderService.com or upon request from the Reader Service.

We make a portion of our mailing list available to reputable third parties that offer products we believe may interest you. If you prefer that we not exchange your name with third parties, or if you wish to clarify or modify your communication preferences, please visit us at www.ReaderService.com/consumerschoice or write to us at Reader Service Preference Service, P.O. Box 9062, Buffalo, NY 14269. Include your complete name and address.

Harlequin *Presents*

Discover an enchanting duet filled with glitz,
glamour and passionate love from

Melanie Milburne

THE *Outrageous* SISTERS

*The twin sisters **everyone's** talking about!*

Separated by secrets…

Having grown up in different families, Gisele and Sienna live lives
that are worlds apart. Then a very public revelation
propels them into the world's eye.…

Drawn together by scandal!

Now the sisters have found each other—but are they at risk of losing
their hearts to the two men who are determined to peel back
the layers of their glittering facades?

Find out in

DESERVING OF HIS DIAMONDS?
Available July 24

ENEMIES AT THE ALTAR
Available August 21

USA TODAY *bestselling author Lynne Graham brings*
you a brand-new story of passion and drama.

THE SECRETS SHE CARRIED

"DON'T play games with me," she urged, breathing in deeply and slowly, nostrils flaring in dismay at the familiar spicy scent of his designer aftershave.

The smell of him, so achingly familiar, unleashed a tide of memories. But Cristo had not made a commitment to her, had not done anything to make her feel secure and had never once mentioned love or the future. At the end of the day, in spite of all her precautions, he had still walked away untouched while she had been crushed in the process.

The knowledge that she had meant so little to him that he had ditched her to marry another woman still burned like acid inside her.

"Maybe I'm hoping you'll finally come clean," Cristo murmured levelly.

Erin turned her head, smooth brow indented with a frown as she struggled to recall the conversation and get back into it again. "Come clean about what?"

Cristo pulled off the road into a layby before he responded. "I found out what you were up to while you were working for me at the Mobila spa."

Erin twisted her entire body around to look at him, crystalline eyes flaring bright, her rising tension etched in the taut set of her heart-shaped face. "What do you mean… what I was up to?"

Cristo looked at her levelly, ebony dark eyes cool and opaque as frosted glass. "You were stealing from me."

"I am not a thief," Erin repeated doggedly, although an alarm bell had gone off in her head the instant he mentioned

the theft and sale of products from the store.

"I have the proof," Cristo retorted crisply. "You can't talk or charm your way out of this, Erin—"

"I'm not interested in charming you. I'm not the same woman I was when we were together," Erin countered curtly, for what he had done to her had toughened her. There was nothing like surviving an unhappy love affair to build self-knowledge and character, she reckoned painfully. He had broken her heart, taught her how fragile she was, left her bitter and humiliated. But she had had to pick herself up again fast once she'd discovered that she was pregnant.

Cristo is going to make Erin pay back what he believes she stole—in whatever way he demands.... But little does he know that Erin's about to drop two very important bombshells!

Pick up a copy of THE SECRETS SHE CARRIED by Lynne Graham, available August 2012 from Harlequin Presents®.

 Harlequin®

ROMANTIC

SUSPENSE

CINDY DEES

takes you on a wild journey to find the truth
in her new miniseries

Code X

Aiden McKay is more than just an ordinary man. As part of
an elite secret organization, Aiden was genetically enhanced
to increase his lung capacity and spend extended time under
water. He is a committed soldier, focused and dedicated
to his job. But when Aiden saves impulsive free spirit
Sunny Jordan from drowning she promptly overturns his
entire orderly, solitary world.

As the danger creeps closer, Adien soon realizes Sunny is the
target…but can he save her in time?

Breathless Encounter

Find out this August!

plus
**BONUS
STORY
INSIDE!**

Look out for a reader-favorite bonus story included in each
Harlequin Romantic Suspense book this August!

www.Harlequin.com

HRS27786